THE DAY OF THE NIGHTFISH

D.T. NEAL

THE DAY OF THE NIGHTFISH

NOSETOUCH PRESS

CHICAGO | PITTSBURGH

THE DAY OF THE NIGHTFISH

© 2020 by D. T. Neal. All Rights Reserved.

ISBN-13: 978-1-944286-14-9

Published by Nosetouch Press
www.nosetouchpress.com

For more information about bulk purchases,
please contact Nosetouch Press at info@nosetouchpress.com.

Cataloging-in-Publication Data

Names: Neal, D.T., author.
Title: The Day of the Nightfish / D.T. Neal
Description: Chicago, IL : Nosetouch Press [2013]
Identifiers: ISBN: 9781944286149 (paperback)
Subjects: LCSH: Horror—Fiction. | Sea monsters—Fiction. |
GSAFD: Horror fiction. | BISAC: FICTION / Horror.

Cover & interior designed by
Christine M. Scott, Clever Crow Consulting and Design
www.clevercrow.com

The text for this book was set in Minion Pro.

For Ian

ONE

DON'T READ THIS THE WRONG WAY,
but if you've ever had nightfish, you'd know just why
I did it. I like to think I've been around the world
enough times, tried my share of delicious delights,
but nightfish, my god: there are no words. And there's
good and bad in that, trust me. It changes you.

I'd first had it while in Phuket with my girlfriend,
Jade Kincaid. Yeah, she's *that* Jade—Jade of JADED
online fame. Maybe she's even influenced you, and
you didn't even know it. She had gotten wind of it
when we were staying at the posh Hotel Elsinore, saw
the words on the menu and almost lost her mind.

Jade played with her lip ring when she told me
about it, this little loop of silver in which she'd set a
tiny black bead that matched her eyes. That month,
her hair was green, long, tied back in a ponytail. People didn't even give it a second glance these days. Her
fans expected it, had buoyed her clicks with their ex-
citement that Jade had gone green. She'd been pink
the year before. Sponsors followed sharklike in her
influential wake. It didn't take much to wind up her
fans, but when she triggered them, they moved wherever she told them to go, and whenever.

"I've heard it's more exotic than anything," Jade said. "*Fugu* is for Boomers."

"What, is it dangerous?" I asked. I liked danger. I liked Jade. We had a thing. It's what we called our relationship—our thing.

"No," she said. "It's delicious. *That's* what people say."

"It's food," I said. I did a lot of different things. I liked it that way. Suppose that made me a dilettante, if only I'd actually been artistic.

I worked on a tuna fishing boat one summer. I tried crab fishing and lobstering one time, as well. I liked to cook, was training (slowly) to be a chef. But for me, there was some fun in working at the front lines of food production, keeping my finger on the culinary pulse—going to the source, seeing for myself, learning. I liked sourcing. I liked knowing. Knowing required doing. Doing meant going to different places and trying different things.

To me, it was like how Hemingway was always going on safaris and fishing—he was a writer, right? So, part of him going out on adventures was a way of him convincing himself that he *wasn't* a pussy. He was a writer, not a matador. But he *wished* he was a matador. I mean, he wanted that, big-time.

It's like when an actor takes up motorcycling, or a musician goes scuba-diving. When you're in the arts, you have to do things like that to level yourself. Maybe to make yourself feel like you're not entirely a fraud. Artists hang back and take it all in. Artists spectate and speculate. Artists who dive in? They don't live too long. Ever noticed that? What makes a great artist is the ability and willingness to *observe,* even more important than participating, when you think about it. Which I did.

And while some people maybe didn't think cooking was an art, that was because most people I knew just shoveled whatever they could grab into their mouths. Most people I knew didn't cook. Didn't know how to, didn't *want* to know. People did not think about what it was they were eating, where it came from, or how it was made.

By some people, you just know I'm talking about Americans. Because that's what I was. It's what Jade was. It's what *we* were. We were Americans. We are Americans. We're American—it works as both an adjective and a noun, man.

I went into the field and did dangerous jobs that were tied to my chosen soon-to-be profession because I needed to see it from front to back, soup to nuts. I needed to know the whole story. You think a pork chop is a pig? Yeah, it's made from pig, but a pig is bigger than bacon, far more than ham. You can't possibly appreciate a good pork chop unless you've seen the pig that it came from. Where it lived, what it ate. Where it grew up. How it lived, how it died. There was a symphony of life behind every food, if you only took the time to look and listen.

Sourcing is everything, like I said. You see where your food comes from, you gain an understanding. Food tastes better when you know where it comes from, when you know what it's been through. That insight matters, whether you realize it or not.

Most people don't want to even think about it. But I did. For me, it wasn't just culinary tourism. For me it was what was going to set me apart from the other wannabes—I wasn't going to be a goddamned cook; I was going to be a motherfucking chef.

And that meant cultivating my palette (and palate) of flavors for my culinary arsenal. It wasn't enough to have a good palate, not anymore—you needed the right tools, secret weapons. I'm not talking gimmicks, special sauces, secret spices; I'm talking mad skills and keen insights. Like deep knowledge.

That's what had Jade and me in Phuket. I'd been chasing down some exotic spices when we'd hit on Elsinore, and Jade, who was fluent in Thai, told me they had nightfish there.

Because I'd been a bit swamped at the time, because I *wasn't* an influencer, I'd not been at ground zero when nightfish had first burst on the scene. I'd been distracted and somehow I'd missed it. It had debuted at Magnifique, a five-star restaurant in New York, late in 2019. The recipe was Nightfish Paillard with Blood Orange. And when I'd heard about it, I'd wondered what it was, right off the bat.

What the hell was it?

Before I knew it, she'd ordered us a plate at $85. Nightfish steak with a coconut curry sauce, served with rice noodles.

"How do you even know about it?" I asked her.

"You know how. I just know things," Jade said. "You'll thank me when you've had it."

Jade smiled with this crooked leer that made everything look like a punch line to a joke only she was in on. It was a game we played with each other. She with me, me with her. Who was on the receiving end of the punch line depended on the moment, setting, situation, and the circumstance. Jade was a masterful counterpuncher, quick on her feet. I respected that about her. Sometimes she'd lead and land one on me. This wasn't one of those moments.

"You don't know," I said, watching crowds mill past the armored windows of Elsinore. "You've never had it, either."

She couldn't debate that because she knew I was right. The waiter came and he put it on a serving dish between us, gave us each a plate, and said something in Thai that Jade answered, and I was none the wiser. Relationships were built on trust, and, despite all we'd been through, I trusted Jade implicitly.

We had an understanding. Part of dating an influencer, like what they never say, is that you come under their influence, yourself. They're good at it. Jade was an enchantress because she was enchanting far more than she was annoying.

The nightfish steak was pretty, plated on a bed of rice noodles arranged to look like clouds. The nightfish itself was green meat with a black skin. The scent was savory, hinting at astringent in the way that seafood sometimes was.

"What the fuck is this?" I asked, poking it with a set of chopsticks.

"It's nightfish, Dummy," Jade said, sniffing the coconut curry sauce. "Mmmm, curry."

"But what *is* it?" I asked, while Jade pried a piece off with her sticks, popped it in her mouth.

"It's delicious," Jade said, all but rolling her eyes. "Ohmigod, yes."

Her face said it all. There is something sublime in another person's enjoyment, and food—good food— is such a primal, essential, personal and shared experience. I could see Jade savoring that first bite, and I halfway resented her for beating me to it. But that's how she rolled. She wasn't training to be a chef. She was trying to be an architect, when she wasn't busy influencing the online world. She understood perspective, but didn't know a thing about food.

She was already grabbing more when I managed to get myself some and took a bite. To say it was delicious was an understatement. Totally not the right way to put it. "Delicious" was an entirely inadequate word for nightfish.

Nightfish was in some exquisitely delectable place between red snapper, ahi tuna, sea bass, swordfish, grouper, and mako. It was almost perfectly between them, equidistant. It was the nexus of those flavors, and something else, something I couldn't define.

Delicate texture: springy, but a perfect mouth feel as that firmness gave way to your teeth, and the flavor of it, at once mild and savory, with the hot kick of the curry balanced by the rich sweetness of the coconut. The meat would rend flawlessly as you chewed, bringing out more subtle gradients of flavor in cascading waves.

I hadn't had anything like it. The way the flesh melted in my mouth, butter-smooth in texture. I even ate some of the skin, the green-black scales, trying to place the flavor. It tasted like nothing I'd ever had before. And I'd had a lot of things in my young life.

"My god," I said, and determined in that instant that I'd try nightfish at every restaurant I found it, because I had to know it intimately.

I could see Jade liking it, too. She took out her phone and filmed herself eating it for JADED.

"Hi, guys, I'm in Phuket, at the Hotel Elsinore with my boy, and I'm totally eating nightfish. It's incredible. So incredibly delicious! And a bargain at $85 a plate! That's over 2700 Baht, in case you wondered."

She uploaded that, quickly took a couple of shots of herself with her food, posing beatifically in front of it. Just like that, uploaded and out there. The likes chimed in, and she muted her phone.

I asked her to ask the waiter where they got it, and she spoke to the waiter, who brought out one of the chefs, who told her that nightfish only came from one place in the world, and it was in the United States.

The United States? What were they even talking about? Nothing exotic came from America. Sure, that was all a matter of perspective, but come on. Beyond inventing eating standing up, what else had we done in the world of cooking? We were a people who lived on fusion cuisine, which by its very nature avoided the exotic. American cooking avoided the risk of being overpowering and alienating. Fusion cuisine got along to get along.

"Seriously?" I asked.

Jade said something else to the chefs, her Thai ricocheting around with theirs, like way too many words for so simple an answer.

"Yeah," Jade said.

"Ohmigod, whatever," I said, and Jade shooed the chef away, who looked over his shoulder once or twice before disappearing in the back.

While Jade was still filling her face, I was using my phone to google "nightfish"—just to see what came up. There were references to it, how it had turned up internationally last year after languishing regionally in New England. Nobody seemed to know where it came from for sure, or what kind of fish it was.

"I can't believe you're not eating this," Jade said, her mouth full of the stuff. "Not that I'm complaining. More for me!"

There was only one registered supplier of it, the Blackfin Fishing Company, based in Gunwale, Rhode Island. Gunwale had been a downtrodden coastal fishing town that had suffered from the collapse in fishing stocks in the wake of global warming.

Unlike some of the other towns that had been able to rebrand themselves as tourist attractions, Gunwale had economically declined until the arrival of Blackfin, which had turned things around for them in a big way. All of it was tied to the production and marketing of nightfish.

"It must be synthetic," I said. "Like imitation crabmeat or something."

"No way," Jade said, giving me hard looks while I treated myself to more of it.

"What?" I asked.

"Don't hog it," Jade said.

"You're the one hogging it," I said.

"Am not," Jade said, and we dueled a moment with our chopsticks, Jade managing to snag another morsel with those deft hands of hers. Undeterred, I went at it while she was chewing.

We devoured the dish in minutes, all but licking the plate clean. I could hear her phone buzzing on the tabletop from the sea of likes rolling in. Her worshippers were already swarming over her post, drinking it in, commenting, living, loving, reveling in Jade's moment.

"That was fantastic," I said. "The supplier for it is in Gunwale."

"Gunwale? Where's that?" Jade asked, licking her fingers with diabolically long strokes of her tongue.

"Rhode Island," I said.

And I didn't even have to say it, because she knew. She understood that I was going to fly my ass to Gunwale and find out about this nightfish.

"Go," she said. "I'm still doing my study on comparative landscaping. I'm not going anywhere."

She made a shooing gesture with her hands, her black-painted nails, fingertips chipped, silver rings on three fingers: a snake, a dragon, and a tiger.

"Not just yet," I said, grabbing her hand.

—

TWO

I LINGERED with Jade in Phuket for three more days, and we had nightfish at three other restaurants, me dragging Jade through town to find it, acting as my translator and navigator.

Jade did photos and posts on it for her fans, and was already forging trend lines with the effortless abandon she brought to everything she did. Whether she was a macro- or micro-influencer was a point of contention between us, and I never pushed the issue.

Some of her rival influencers were doing their own posts about nightfish, naturally, like wherever they were. But because Jade had gotten ahead of them on JADED, they were playing catch-up, which meant trying to either outdo her own exotic locale in Thailand or else pivot short attention spans to new distractions. Veganna Karenina, one of Jade's rivals, was already complaining about the sourcing of nightfish, suggested some viable non-meat alternatives to it using some sort of processed green soy food paste from Veganation.

During that time, I'd tried to identify it, but nobody knew what the hell nightfish actually was. A food scientist named Martin Munser had done some genetic sequencing of samples of it and said that it appeared to be a kind of amphibian or reptile, but of undetermined origin.

"You know, maybe it's a bug," Jade said.

"Bugs aren't amphibians or reptiles," I said. Not like I wanted to quibble with Jade, but precision in taxonomy and nomenclature mattered, at least to me.

"You know what I mean," Jade said. She'd been painting her nails while we were at the hotel. Jade hadn't wanted to stay in some seedy hotel during her study, so she tapped her folks and had them book her for a month at the Elsinore.

She could have paid for it herself, but leaning on the folks fit the whole co-dependent dynamic she had with them. Her folks disapproved of her social media influencer lifestyle, kept hammering on her to get her degree in architecture sorted out, just for when JADED flamed out. The nice thing about five-star living in Thailand was that it was affordable. The Baht wasn't yet the dollar, lucky for us.

"Here's the thing," I said. "If it's a reptile, why the fuck call it 'nightfish?'"

"You're the chef, you figure it out. You tell me," Jade said, between smooth strokes of nail enamel. She had such steady hands. I think she got that from her father, who was a neurosurgeon. Jade had played piano as a girl. Her folks had made her take lessons, although she'd never cared about it that much.

From my own workplace meanderings, I knew a little something about the marketing of foods. Not from a strategic or campaign perspective, mind you. More like from a frontline vantage point, like in the trenches, where it really mattered. Sometimes you had to come up with evocative names to sell something, like mahi mahi, canola oil, sea bass, and orange roughy. "Nightfish" was clearly one of those cases when the marketing department at Blackfin had gone to work coming up with an evocative name for it.

Almost nobody wanted to eat a lizard, I supposed. It was one of those things that just wasn't done. People understood "fish" and liked it. Maybe that was all it took—a few words people could recognize, and there it was.

"Hey, maybe it's some kind of sea snake," I said. "Like a sea serpent."

"Oooh. Only I really don't think sea serpents are *real,* Babe," Jade said, blowing on her fingertips, although I could see she didn't care. She liked the nightfish.

However, for her, it was already being filed away in that architect's brain of hers, going into deep storage. It had been an experience, but the experience was already shelved in the past. Food was food, and Jade was JADED. Her influencer frenemies and rivals were already moving on to other things, and Jade was, too. It was one part gamesmanship, one part affectation, one part survival.

After several nights of nightfish, I could see she was already sailing way past it. That was just Jade. Jade would get bored. *Moments* mattered to Jade, but that's all they ever were. A stack of moments, the building blocks of a memory, and nothing more. Jade and I had shared a mountain of moments together. In retrospect, I always felt like they meant more to me than to her.

Me, I was transfixed by the piquant subtlety of the flavor. Maybe "obsession" is too weighty a word for it, but I *felt* a bit obsessed about it. I was the type of guy who traveled from enthusiasm to enthusiasm, wherever it took me.

I had to try it in other settings. Like places other than Thailand (no offense). Different restaurants. I borrowed some money from Jade and booked a plane flight to Hawaii, where I stayed overnight, had Grilled Nightfish Kebabs with ginger and onions at the Tsunami Lounge, and marveled at the taste and texture of it, how it lent itself so readily to another interpretation. That astringent bite was in there, offset by the tang of the ginger and onions.

Then I flew from Hawaii to San Francisco, had Nightfish Cioppino at The Hotel Argent. Again, it was delicious. Different, and yet consistent. Unique and familiar. However it was dressed up, nightfish never let you forget what it was—even if you didn't know what it was.

At each venue, I would send Jade a picture of me trying the entrée, and she'd just text back how silly I was, how cutely obsessed I'd get about things. She was still studying transformative landscapes, in between taking pictures of herself in Thailand, posing in a saffron bikini with a sponsor's coconut oil-infused CBD body balm.

I flew cross-country, got myself to Gunwale, which itself was a travel adventure I won't bore you with. Just know that, eventually, after renting a car in Providence, I drove down to Gunwale, where I hunted down the mysterious Blackfin Fishing Company. I'd done my research on the trip east.

Gunwale itself was one of those almost entirely utilitarian New England coastal towns that were probably never quite charming in their long history, although they had somehow managed to be quaint. You could almost see the ghosts of the Puritan founders of Gunwale glowering at you from the old buildings.

But there was money here, all the same. I could see it in the new paint jobs on the handful of taverns and restaurants I went past as I drove down the main street. This was a company town. I could see the Blackfin logo on trucks driving past me—a black circle on a field of white with a black fin in the center like a shark's fin, with the company name below it.

Blackfin was a new company. It had originally been Bellview & Oakum, a partnership between a ship owner, Phil Bellview, and one of the only remaining successful area fishermen, Bob Oakum. They'd worked together for over 15 years. Oakum was the face of Blackfin, while Bellview was the bankroll.

The Blackfin Fishing Company was something they put together in 2010. As it was, Bellview & Oakum had owned a section of Gunwale wharves and warehouses, which had become Blackfin property. The whole place was razor-fenced in, and the Blackfin logo was all over it. It looked like an Army base, in a way. Blandly unwelcoming, designed to be functional, even if you weren't intended to understand what those functions were.

Walking along the fenced barricade, I could see a dozen fishing boats moored, all of them sporting the company flag. The boats looked different from any fishing boats I'd ever seen. They were low-slung and broad-beamed. It made me think that these trawlers weren't ideally suited for deep sea voyages, but likely hugged the coast, or at least didn't stray too far from it. They looked like gunboats, only they didn't have any guns.

There was also a certain ruggedness to their design—they may have been built for shallow waters, but they were very sturdily constructed, I could tell. You could just see it in the size of the boats and the taut steel construction. They looked like a fusion between a fishing boat and a Coast Guard cutter, if such a thing made sense.

I went to the security guard post that was at the entry gate to Blackfin. The attending guard, a burly guy with short black hair and a mustache, got up at my approach, arms crossed.

"What can I do for you, Sir?" he asked.

"I was wondering, is this the place that catches nightfish?"

"That depends," the guard said. His nametag said his name was Tony. "Are you a reporter?"

"No," I said. "I'm looking for work."

It was a whimsical decision, something I just pulled squarely out of my ass. But I was a big guy, young and strong. Opportunities were there for the opportunistic. I was nothing, if not opportunistic.

Tony the Guard looked me over with a smirk and said "Yeah? They're always needing fresh blood in there."

"It's that rough, huh?"

Tony shrugged. "Let's just say I'm glad I'm over here and not out there."

He jabbed a thumb seaward. Sea life wasn't for everybody. Even I knew that, and I had only dipped my toes in it a few times. There was a power and purity in it, but it was always dangerous. The ocean was like that. As beautiful as it was, as full of life as it was, it was deadly dangerous, and if you ever forgot that, it would forcefully remind you.

"So, can I go in?"

"Not a chance," Tony said. "They don't take walk-ins at Blackfin. You got to go through the system."

"Which is what, exactly?"

"HR, background checks, that kind of thing," Tony said. "It's a process."

I looked past him, to the warehouses and processing and distribution stations. Tony watched me watching, cleared his throat.

"Look, you gotta log in and deal with HR," he said. "They want to know that you can read and write. No criminal record, liability waivers, and so on."

"What's that got to do with fishing?"

Tony shrugged. "I don't make the rules. And they don't take walk-ins."

"Alright," I said, left him alone, walked away from the front gate, mulled through my options.

I didn't know anybody in Gunwale, so I called up Jade, after texting to see if she was around. It was half-past noon in Gunwale, which meant it was like almost midnight in Phuket, so Jade was up, since she kept architect's hours, when she wasn't primping-n-pimping on JADED.

"What?" she asked. "Did you find your nightfish?"

"I'm right at the factory," I said. "It's, like, across the street from me. I snapped a picture with my phone, sent it to her.

"Ohmigod," Jade said. "That looks even more boring than I could have imagined."

"I'm trying to get a job there," I said.

"Oh, jeez," she said. "Why are you calling me, Babe?"

"Can I borrow some more money? I'll pay you back," I said. "I just need a place to stay while I try to get a job with these guys."

I could see her in my head, playing with her lip ring, thinking it over. We both knew she had the money. JADED made her a lot of money, like her various sponsorships. They kept her well-heeled, above and beyond whatever she scored from her rich, half-assed helicopter parents.

"I'm good for it, you know that," I said. "Just put it on my tab."

"If you get a job there, I'm so garnishing your wages," Jade said. It was easy for Jade to say; she'd never actually had a real job, like ever. "I'll send you some money. But you owe me."

"Thanks, Baby," I said. "Miss you."

I hung up and walked around Gunwale, which, aside from the Blackfin Fishing Company, was little more than a reasonably picturesque little fishing town that had a local grocery store, a hardware store, and a dozen bars and taverns. There was a motel and a single, white-painted church. The church looked old, although it had been recently painted, and was gleaming bone white.

I checked my account and saw that Jade had wired me some money, and got myself a room at the Blackfin Motel, where I'd go later to crash. The young woman at the front desk just looked at me with bemusement. She had brown hair and looked younger than me, but the noncommittal frown made her seem older, more responsible—not by choice, but by necessity. She raked me with her mud-brown eyes, a sidelong and suspicious gaze. Her nametag said she was Olivia.

"You're here for, what? Getting a job, maybe?" Olivia asked.

"For sure, yeah," I said.

"Good luck," she said, handing me my keys, which had a navy blue plastic plaque upon which a white anchor had been emblazoned, with the motel's name on it and phone number. "People come and go in Gunwale. And, you know, sometimes they don't come back, the ones who go to sea."

"Is that so?" I asked. She looked nervous that I even replied, despite her initiating the conversation. I affected a blasé vibe, to put her at ease. "Dangerous work, is it?"

"Uh, yeah," she said. "Really dangerous. That's what jacks up the prices for it. We pay for nightfish in Gunwale blood around here. But we get something back for it. Blackfin's been good to Gunwale."

Her eyes flitted over me a moment, then around the room, but we were alone. The town was hardly crowded this time of day.

"Have you ever seen one?" I asked.

"Like wild caught?" she replied. "Nope. Seen the jaws. Some folks have the jaws around their places. You know, like trophies."

"Yeah," I said.

"But Blackfin's real quiet about them," she said. "The boats head out at night, and they usually come back at dawn, when everybody's sleeping. They make the workers at the factory sign NDAs. Blackfin pays well, though. So keeping quiet seems like a small price to pay."

Nondisclosure agreements seemed weird to me. Whatever their secret was, Blackfin sure didn't want anybody getting in on it. My chances of getting to the bottom of things were probably more remote than ever.

"I get that," I said. "Do you know anywhere I might go to get work on a boat?"

Olivia looked at me and shrugged, like she was sloughing off the weight of the world.

"You don't want to work on a boat," she said. "I mean, you really don't. The factory's where you want to try your luck."

She didn't know me or particularly care about me, but I could tell she was sincere in her concern. It was all but tattooed on her face.

"Why not a boat?"

"I mean, you're big enough," Olivia said. "Let me see your hands."

I held them out, and she took them in her hands, turned them over.

"Soft hands," she said. "Unscarred. Best keep them that way."

"I have scars," I said. I pulled out of her grasp, more out of freshly wounded pride than anything else.

"Not *real* scars," Olivia said.

"Real enough. I've done real work," I said.

"Not recently," she said. "Look, the boat crews are their own thing. The factory's where you want to go. They'd take you there, provided you don't talk too much."

I balled my soft hands into fists. While she wasn't wrong that it had been awhile since I had worked a rough job, I'd done more than my share of time in honest labor.

"What if I felt compelled to try to land work on a boat? Where would I go? Who would I talk to?"

Olivia looked around like she was sharing some deep secret, before leaning in.

"I'd check with Captain Noah Wayland," Olivia said. "Of the *Amanda Luce*. He's one of the best skippers out there, and they're always needing crew. But he'd never take you on."

"Why not?" I asked. Olivia's matter-of-fact dismissals were wounding me. Did I look so babyfaced? I mean, what the hell?

"Most of the nightfish boats avoid greenhorns," Olivia said. "Except for chum, maybe."

"Where would I find him?" I asked.

"The crew of the Mandy frequent the Thirsty Mermaid, right next door to Swallows Tavern and Wenchies' Bar-N-Grille." Olivia said. "Most of the crews show up there eventually. If you're seriously determined to try to get on a 'fishboat, I'd say that's the place to go. Just don't tell them that I pointed you there. And don't tell Noah I sent you."

I laughed, and Olivia just gazed sourly at me a moment.

"Don't worry, I won't ruin your reputation," I said. "Tell me where I can find this Thirsty Mermaid."

—

THREE

OLIVIA DIDN'T steer me wrong. The Thirsty Mermaid had this golden, buxom mermaid perched on a hand-painted sign. She held one beer aloft, was guzzling the other with a gape-mouthed grin, beer splashing down her scaly bosom. She winked at me.

The predominant color scheme of the place was green and gold, and there was next to nobody inside. I saw only a thirtysomething redheaded bartender chick and a couple of locals at the bar. Everybody had the same dour look about them that Olivia had been sporting.

"What'll you have?" she asked.

"Whatever you have on tap," I said.

The bar was mostly old wood and mirrors. Over the bar was a pair of jaws mounted on a plaque. About as wide across as a basketball, the teeth about an inch long, triangular. The wide set of the jaws didn't look familiar to me.

"What kind of shark is that?"

"It's not a shark," the bartender said. "That's a night-fish."

"Never heard of a nightfish," I said. Sometimes, it paid off to play dumb. Especially in places like this. When you played dumb, people talked, because they weren't threatened by you. People would talk to idiots without fear of consequences. So, I played the fool more often than not.

The locals, one a fat older man with a faded red baseball cap jammed on his head, another an even older guy who looked like he was made of nicotine and old newspaper. His hair was snow white.

"That's because there's no such thing," the old man said.

"Harvey," the bartender said. "Harvey" looked at me with the palest blue eyes, watery from whiskey. His face was old leather, wrinkled and weatherworn beyond imagining.

If I ever looked that old, I'd throw myself into the sea, my ankle strapped to an anchor. There was no coming back from that kind of aging, no possibility of rehabilitation. I could only imagine what Jade might think, seeing that man's wizened face. She'd get one of her skin cream sponsors to ship her a case of moisturizer, just on general principles.

"Rose won't have me saying it, but I've got the right of it," Harvey said. "It's just a name for what's out there."

"I'm looking for work at Blackfin," I said.

The locals snorted, and Rose just shook her head. Their eyes danced with each other, and I knew there was something there, a story to be told, or one they were hell-bent on not telling me. For me, that's all I needed to goad me on.

"What for?" she said.

"For money, of course," I said. "I need a job."

They looked at one another again, like I'd said something crazy. I looked up at the skeletal maw of the thing, thought it was impressive, for sure, could take a bad bite out of a man, but it couldn't be much worse than a shark or a barracuda.

I mean, that was bad enough, and that skeletal jaw would have put the hurt on me. I imagined what that would be like, those jaws clamped on my leg, my forearm, my chest. Yeah, that would hurt. Maybe it would even kill. Who was I kidding? Yeah, it would kill the hell out of me, depending where the bite came down. I tried not to think of that nasty thing biting me at all. Your life went where your mind took you, and I wasn't about to take myself to that dark place.

"The security guard said they needed people here all the time," I said.

Harvey coughed into his hand. "Looks like it, sure enough. Fishing's dangerous work. And there's nothing more dangerous than nightfishing."

I looked him squarely in the eye, while Harvey tried to avoid my gaze.

"Have you seen them?"

"I worked in the processing plant," Harvey said. "That's all I know. They make us sign gag orders at Blackfin."

"Pipe down, Harvey," the fat guy said. "Have another drink, why don't you?"

"Trade secrets," I said. "NDAs. I get it."

Olivia had nothing to worry about. I wasn't going to let on that she'd directed me here. But the locals at the bar were singing the same tune. They were all edgy, and that made me edgy, too.

I was one of those types of people who soaked up the vibe of my surroundings like a sponge. It meant I was great fun at parties, and a good wingman in a fight. I could read the room, and I would give back as good as I got, more often than not.

The fat guy poked me in the chest with a finger.

"Listen, Kid. You don't want to go out on one of those boats."

With these guys talking the way they were, you think I wanted to turn my tail and leave Gunwale? I was determined I'd get out on one of those boats. This was fucking happening. Jade would understand. I mean, some things you just *had* to do. You knew them when you saw them. This was one of those moments.

The locals could see it on my face. I wasn't going to be deterred. The locals looked at me with some blend of bitter contempt and knowing sorrow. These were people who'd been through things, and maybe because I was young, they both wanted to shield me from those things, and also felt irritation at my youthful belief that I could take anything that was thrown my way.

I could just see it in their faces, and in their eyes. The way they grimaced, and the hint of frowns that hung at the edge of even their nervous smiles. It was that Gunwale Look the locals had about them. There was a distinctive kind of expression they all had: fear, paranoia, contempt, pride, bitterness, and something else I couldn't quite make out.

"Sure, Kid," the fat guy said. "I know. You think you can just go out there and know what you're doing? Just like that?"

"Were you out there?" I asked. The fat guy shook his head. "Oh, hell, no. I just worked in the packing plant."

"So, none of you guys really knows what you're talking about, am I right?"

The fat guy wrinkled his nose. "We know more than you, Kid. And we know better than the talk about it. Blackfin's got lawyers, they have investigators. Nobody in Gunwale talks about it."

"Why the big secret?" I asked, getting sick of how cryptic everybody was being. Maybe they wanted to protect me, but at some point, that chafes your pride. I'd seen plenty of things in my life already. I was more than ready for the nightfish. "Who cares? It's fish."

"It ain't no fish," Harvey said, but the others glared at him, and he quieted, looking down at his feet. He muttered to himself, and I couldn't tell if he was chastened or sullen. He sailed between those two poles, stepping from one foot to the other, like he was dancing a miserable little hornpipe.

"I'm looking for Captain Wayland of the *Amanda Luce*," I said, which made the regulars positively twitchy.

"You know him?" the fat guy asked.

"I know of him," I said. "His reputation."

"What do you know?" Harvey said, practically spitting whiskey at me.

"I know he takes on crewmen," I said.

"Not greenhorns," the fat guy said. "You're about as green as they come, Kid."

Just then a group of big men came lumbering into the bar, slamming their way in past the doors. There was a couple dozen of them, all of them looking like they were a hybrid of hockey players and football players—big, broad-shouldered, large- and hard-handed. All of them wore jeans and flannel shirts of various plaid patterns, and most of them wore baseball caps or stocking caps. Most were bearded. Their eyes were harder than their hands, by the look of them. They piled onto the bar, lined up, and Rose served them up beers with a gap-toothed, not unbecoming grin.

I looked at these men, who were somewhere between my age and maybe ten years older, weatherworn and aged by hard labor, faces blank, muttering to each other and lighting up cigarettes by the handful. They smelled of sea salt, wool, sweat, and smoke.

"Hey, fellas," Harvey said. "This kid wants to go nightfishin' with you on the Mandy."

Several of them looked me up and down, and I felt self-conscious in the face of their mute surveillance. This group of men were more a pack than any sort of human gathering. The feral life that bound them was unmistakable. These were men who had seen and known things I could not yet hope to comprehend. They were brothers in arms. Like soldiers, maybe. Veterans.

One of them, the nearest one, a young guy with wild brown hair that sprayed out from under his cap, just laughed. "Babyface McGee, here?"

"I've worked on a tuna boat, a swordfish boat, and crab and lobster boats," I said, feeling more than a little defensive. Yeah, these were big, tough guys, but I was a big, tough guy, too. Hell, I played rugby in college. Anybody who played rugby knew what tough was. That's what I told myself. I hadn't been in the service, hadn't fought any war in Afghanistan or Iraq, but I'd done things, all the same.

Another of them, a tall guy with broad shoulders and several scars across his face, these smooth white lines of creased and dimpled flesh that contrasted with his sunburn-pink skin and his black beard and blue eyes, looked at me with withering scorn.

"This is nothing like that," he said. "Not even close."

"C'mon," I said. "Give me a shot."

The Skipper spoke. I knew he was their captain by the deference his men gave him. He was this red-haired guy with a lantern jaw and brown eyes, freckles across the bridge of his nose. He was wearing a midnight blue ribbed turtleneck, black jeans, and a brown leather jacket so worn and cracked as to appear to be some kind of hide he'd cobbled together.

"Why are you so eager to go nightfishing?" he asked. "You look like you could almost be smart. Like you could be doing something else with your life. You think these clowns here are doing this because they *want* to?"

I looked at the men, half of whom were looking back witheringly at me, the other half were just concentrating on their drinks and talking to each other, as if I was beneath their notice, unworthy of even a lick of their time or attention. I could see Rose, Harvey, and the fat man watching, as well—spectating, more like. It was probably more entertainment than they'd seen in Gunwale for a long time.

"He's a tourist," the shaggy-haired guy said.

"He came looking for you, Captain," Harvey said, earning a rib poke from the fat guy.

"Oh, he did, did he?" the Skipper said. "That true, Kid?"

"Yeah," I said. "I heard that you're one of the best nightfish captains out there. If you're Captain Wayland, that is."

The Skipper smirked.

"I am," he said. "Who told you about me?"

"Can't say," I said. "But you're a regular Captain Stormalong, if what I've heard was true."

Captain Stormalong was the Pecos Bill of the sea—a giant seafaring legend out of Massachusetts who battled the Kraken and performed a host of seaside feats of almost ludicrous audacity and daring.

"That so?" Wayland asked. "Well, I've had my moments."

His crewmen snickered and ribbed each other, and they looked at me like I was so much fish bait. The look was unmistakable—mocking, contemptuous, condescending. But Wayland was thinking things over, while I was trying to figure out what to say next.

"Still, with Gary gone under, we *are* short a man," one of them said.

Captain Wayland just looked me hard in the face. There was no judgment in his gaze, only a flavor of sadness I'd never seen in a man before. He looked like the faces of men who'd been to war, like the battle-fatigued souls staring forlornly out at you in black and white photographs from World War II or Vietnam.

All of the men had those hard-yet-wounded eyes, despite the boozy camaraderie. All of them looked more than a little weary and even, I have to admit, frightened. That fear was contagious. Although I was not in danger in that old bar, I felt afraid, all the same. If these men were fearful, then I should be afraid, too. Not part of their pack, but still a human animal. We knew fear, carried a tribal comprehension of it, a species memory. That fear was here, with us, in the room. Where it came from was itself a frightening prospect.

"Blackfin screens its night fishermen," Wayland said. "We couldn't bring you on even if we wanted to. Not officially."

"Look, what is the big damned deal? Let me guess, Blackfin made you sign NDAs, too."

The men who heard me looked at each other and laughed, nodding. Despite their laughter, I could see the wariness about them. It hung like the salt, sweat, and acrid nightfish smell they all had about them.

"Damned right they did," Wayland said. "We make a good living doing this, and the last thing we need is some fool greenhorn coming aboard to get himself killed, thinking he's going to, I don't know, prove himself out there? There's nothing out there to prove."

"We could chop him up for bait," the shaggy-haired guy said. "Or hang him from a hook."

"Your ship—"

"My boat," Wayland said, emphasizing the word. "Is the *Amanda Luce.*"

Upon hearing the name of their boat, several of the men did halfhearted toasts, raising their glasses of beer and clanking them together. More fishermen and sailors were entering the bar, even though, by my measure, it was maybe two in the afternoon.

The wild-haired guy even broke out into a song, swiftly joined by his shipmates. They did a little swaying dance as they sang it:

"You're better off putting your neck in a noose
Than serving aboard the Amanda Luce"

Wayland smirked at his men, swatting at the shaggy-haired one, while they mangled more verses.

*"The nightfish know that we're heading to war
And tonight they'll try to settle the score*

*"But Captain Wayland keeps them at bay
If they swim too close he'll make them pay"*

They got more drinks and others joined in their song, dissolving into a chorus of drunken singing and gusty laughter. Wayland seemed pleased by their carrying on, looked at me over his cup.

"Can't you make an exception? Can't you wrangle something to get me aboard? I can help you guys. I'll do anything you need," I said. "And I won't breathe a word of it to anybody."

"Yeah, right," the shaggy-haired guy said. "Skip, this greenhorn's just a wannabe."

"I'll sign a nondisclosure agreement, whatever it takes," I said. "I just want to see it. I've tasted nightfish. I want to know what it is."

When some of the men had heard me say that, they stopped singing, got silent, were glowering at me. I could feel the heat of their gaze, the leaden weight of their disapproval. Somehow, I'd crossed a line with them. That it was a breach of etiquette may have put too fine a point on it, but I'd somehow wronged them with that admission.

"You hear that? The kid's eaten it," the shaggy-haired guy said. "He's a connie-sewer."

"You've eaten it?" Wayland said, laughing bitterly to himself. "You got a taste for it, and you want to see what it is?"

"Yes," I said. "Hell, yes. You mean you guys haven't ever had it?"

"Hell, no," the shaggy-haired guy said. "Nobody in their right mind eats it. Nobody who knows. Nobody in Gunwale touches the stuff."

I held up a hand, because it was pissing me off and I wanted them to stop fronting with me. "You assholes fish for this stuff, then these assholes ashore process and pack it, and it's fucking delicious, and not one of you has tried it?"

Wayland glanced at his men, cleared his throat. "It's valuable stuff. Primo price per pound, you know. Our job is just bringing it in. We're not going to eat into our profits. People pay dearly to eat it. Blackfin pays us to reel it in. So, we provide for the hungry mouths out there. Mouths like yours."

"Besides," the shaggy-haired guy said. "We are up to our waists in the shit. We live and breathe nightfish every night, during the season. The last thing on Earth that any of us want is to eat the fuckers."

"What is wrong with it?" I asked.

"Nothing," Captain Wayland said, when nobody else would. "Nothing at all. Nightfish has been great for Gunwale. Before this came, we'd been sliding into the sea. Nobody comes here. We're not Newport. We're not Providence. We don't have what they do. Gunwale needs this. Blackfin saved this town. The nightfish made us."

I could see the others listening to Captain Wayland. He had that way about him, that presence and natural commanding spirit. He didn't even have to yell. I could tell that his men loved him and listened to him. I didn't have any doubt that they would die for him. Some of them, the ones who weren't there, already had. He carried their ghosts with him, in his wake. He felt every one. I could tell this.

I considered myself a good judge of character, and I could see that Captain Wayland had character. He wasn't some craven opportunist, or some greedy sea baron. He was something else. He was a sea captain. That mattered to him, and it mattered to his men. They depended on each other. Whatever nightfishing precisely was, it mattered to them a great deal.

Seeing that almost gave me pause. I felt like an intruder into this very insular, isolated world. I did not belong here in Gunwale, in the Thirsty Mermaid, talking to this crew. They knew it, and I knew it. Everybody felt it.

But feeling something and being held captive to that feeling was something else. I knew that you had to pry yourself loose of your expectations and inhibitions if you were to go anywhere in life and do anything that mattered to you. This was one of those moments, and I would not relent.

"We get fresh blood in here every season," Captain Wayland said. "Every season they come, sometimes every day, during high time. And every season we need them. But even then, we don't let just anybody in on this. Let me see your hands."

Christ, another hand examination. It had been bad enough when Olivia did it. It would be twice as bad with Wayland, but I knew to demur would make me look like I had something to hide from them, so I did as he commanded.

I held them out, and the Skipper looked them over, turned them over, then back again. I was proud of the various chef scars I had on them, felt like they gave my hands some character. But I could see, especially compared with the hard, scarred, callused hands of Wayland, that, by comparison, they were soft.

"What are you, really? These *aren't* fisherman's hands," Wayland said, tossing my hands back to me like he was lobbing an unwanted catch back into the sea.

"I'm a chef," I said. That made the shaggy-haired guy laugh out loud, all but choking on his beer.

"A chef," he said. "Oh, that's rich. Skip, he wants to make Nightfish Remoulade. Am I right, Kid? Am I right?"

"I want to know what it is, yes," I said. "It was delicious. I want to know."

"He wants to know," the shaggy-haired guy said. "You know, we *could* use a cook aboard the Mandy, Skip."

The Skipper looked hard at me, nodded to himself. "You want to know? I mean, you *really* want to know? Alright. You know what? Get yourself a dinghy and you come aboard when we've left the harbor. He scratched out a phone number on a cocktail napkin, handed it to me.

"Thanks—"

"Don't thank me just yet," Captain Wayland said. "There's no way Blackfin's going to let you board from the company docks, so you take a dinghy out past Sterner Point, where the lighthouse is. You go out there, past the harbor tomorrow at sunset. You call me on your phone, and we'll have the Mandy come pick you up. Now, once you're aboard, no bullshit. You just stay the hell out of everybody's way. I don't want you up in the wheelhouse; I've got enough to worry about.

And if you're with *Rolling Stone* or something, I swear to fucking god I'll feed you to the nightfish, myself. You breathe a word about this, and we're turning you to bait."

"Tomorrow night. Not a word. I got it," I said, pocketing the phone number.

"Not a word," Wayland said. And he looked at everybody nearby who'd been eavesdropping, and said it once again. Then he threw a hundred on the bar and bought everybody a round of drinks, including me.

We drank, and then we drank again, and again, until I lost count.

—

FOUR

HUNG OVER OR NOT, you would think it would be a cinch to charter a dinghy in Rhode Island. You'd think that, but not in Gunwale. When I went to the first guy and asked, this chinless, goggle-gazed crustacean of a man with a comb-over looked at me like I was nuts. He actually stared at me open-mouthed, willing the words to come out of his gullet.

"You want what?"

"I want a dinghy," I said. "A zodiac. Whatever you have for rent. This is a boat rental place, yes?"

"Sure, Mister, but we don't let people charter boats after dark. Not here in Gunwale," he said.

"Let me guess: on account of the nightfish?"

His already large eyes went as big as billiard balls when I'd said that. "Yessir. The liability's just too great for something like that."

Disappointed, I left him sputtering. I went to three places for it, and came up with nothing each time. Nobody would rent me a dinghy for the night. For the day, sure, but not for the night. None of them had seen any nightfish, either; but they were plenty scared of them. The fear was soaked into the bones of everyone in Gunwale, it seemed. It galled me.

What the fuck, right? I mean, Gunwale was small, it was isolated. I got that. But it wasn't run-down. Clearly, people had money in their pockets, and yet they were so scared.

I don't know what was driving that. Like they were scared of the nightfish, and/or scared that maybe the money they'd been making from the nightfish trade would run out or something. I couldn't read it, exactly. Gunwale wasn't a boom town. But it *was* a one-industry town. I guess that was part of it. People were wary of rocking the boat. If Blackfin ever moved out of town or shut down, that would be it for Gunwale. It might as well sink into the sea, if Blackfin went away.

I couldn't live that way. Maybe that's what hobbled me in life, maybe why I was trying to become a chef. I felt like at least as a chef, I'd have cultivated some kind of expertise and would become an intrinsic source of value. As a chef, though, I wasn't captive to the ingredients of what I cooked. My skill, my experience, my imagination, my vision—*that* would be my signature dish. I wasn't an artist, but I would bring something special to the table.

Whereas, for the Gunwale people, their lives were bound up entirely in the nightfish. Maybe it was like the way it was in coal towns—people depended on that coal, even though it killed them. The consensus around the nightfish was fear. That was the only thing I was certain of.

At the fourth place, Lou's Cruises, I just asked to charter a dinghy for the day, having learned my lesson. Lou, who was incredibly tan and had grey-white hair, squinted at his watch and looked me over with his sun-dried raisin gaze.

"It's three o'clock now, Mister. Boat's due back by six o'clock, sharp. No exceptions. It's double the rental fee every hour after sunset. And if you don't mind me saying, you'd be a damned fool to be out in those waters after sunset, anyway."

I nodded and smiled, told Lou that I'd be happy to get the boat back in time, without, of course, any intention of doing so. Tourists got lost all the time. I'd just "get lost" and get the boat back later.

Besides, Jade was paying for it. No worries. She had me covered. It was nice to have that in my back pocket. It wasn't quite insurance, but it was close enough to count.

Lou took Jade's money and he walked me down the wharf to where he kept his dinghies, asked me what I planned to be doing out there. I told him I was nature photographer and wanted to capture some scenic views of Gunwale as part of a New England photo essay I was doing. Lou just listened politely, as if he couldn't imagine anyone bothering to photograph Gunwale like that. He didn't even ask me where my photography gear was.

"Beachfront's not for walking," Lou said. "Those shorelines are off-limits. Seabird rookeries and the like. Off limits."

"Can't hurt to take a look," I said.

"Off-limits, like I said. Storms come in," Lou said. "Waves and wind. Nobody in their right mind would land on the beach. Not in Gunwale. Not this time of year, anyhow."

"What's special about this time of year?" I asked.

Lou looked me over again, pausing before replying. The Gunwale Look cut through a person, in a way. It was an assessment, an appraisal, and a judgment all rolled up in one scathing gaze.

"Nightfish breeding season," Lou said. "They're busy this time of year. Best stay off the beaches, above and beyond regulations."

"I'd still like to take a look," I said.

Lou seemed resigned to my decision, picked out the dinghy for me, had me fill out the paperwork, made sure I had a life vest and an oar. He also handed me a flare, said if I needed help, I could use it.

"Only one oar?" I asked.

"All you need," Lou said. "In case you get stuck out there."

"I don't plan on getting stuck."

"Gets black as pitch after dark," Lou said. "Black as the devil's heart. You get my boat back intact, or there'll be hell to pay. You hear me?"

"I hear you," I said.

Lou didn't seem convinced.

"And back before sunset, above all," he said.

"What happens after sunset?" I asked.

Lou seemed to sense my line of inquiry, and wasn't about to be drawn out into some sort of disclosure he didn't want to share. Least of all to some out-of-towner. Native Gunwale folks knew better, it seemed.

"You just get the dinghy back is all," Lou said. "All you need to know."

"Alright," I said. "I will."

I got into the dinghy, which was named "Silky," and started up the outboard motor. After a couple of tugs on the pull chain, the motor started right up, and the battered blue dinghy and I were gliding away from Lou's and out into the harbor.

From where I was, the view of and perception of Gunwale changed a bit. Long ago, Gunwale had been a British colonial naval outpost, Fort Sterner. The town had arisen to provide needful services to the soldiers and sailors who manned it. Once the Colonies rebelled and became the United States, Fort Sterner had been abandoned and had given itself over to maritime trade.

But the old martial bones of the town could be better seen from the sea. There was no beach in town. Within the harbor walls, it might as well have been a fortress still. There was a sense of enclosure, a feeling like one was about to be crushed in the fist of a giant, as the knot of wharves and piers and seawalls offered a degree of protection from the might of the sea.

I cleared the harbor, passing the Blackfin Fishing Company docks, my eyes raking over the dozen battered and bruised metal boats that made up her fishing fleet. Despite being painted bright red or blue or green, the boats' hulls were crisscrossed with scratches that had cut through the paint, baring the raw steel of the ship. Older scratches had gone to rust, while newer ones were shiny and metallic, still. Fresh wounds on the boats, not yet scabbed over.

There was more than a little satisfaction in this enterprise: I had been successful in my plan so far to find out just what the nightfish was. It was so going to be worth it. I could hardly wait to see Jade, to tell her all about it.

I'd peeked on her feed, and she was still sunbathing in Phuket, peddling some sun lotion slathered on her body. Her sponsors always kept her well-stocked with product that she could push, wherever she was. With her green hair and tanned skin, she looked other-worldly, like a cybernetic sea nymph. I liked her photos, watched the comments pile up from her obsessive fans and followers—an avalanche of adoration. It had to be nice to be so loved, even as shallowly as social media allowed. Jade bathed in the attention of her fans and followers, was marinated remotely in their electronic esteem.

As I sped my rental boat out of the harbor, catching the waves, I felt particularly good in that moment. There was a genuine satisfaction in seeing something through the way I had. I'd jetted across half the planet to make this happen. That meant something to me.

I had already resolved to make Jade a necklace out of some nightfish teeth, if I happened to be lucky enough to get my hands on some. Not a souvenir—souvenirs were for tourists. No, those teeth would be something else: trophies. Jade would appreciate a good trophy, I just knew it. At least for a little while. Or, if I'd really nailed it, it would become part of her permanent rotation, something she'd casually wear day to day.

I got out past Sterner Point, beyond the red and white lighthouse. It looked like a chubby candy cane amid the sand dunes and sea oats. The fishy-salty wind blew strongly out of the sheltering reach of Gunwale's harbor, the sea dark blue and flecked with white foam.

Glancing at the time, I saw it was way too late to talk to Jade. She'd be asleep by now, or would be partying. Maybe both. I texted her, kept it short and sweet, a blown kiss, carried across space and time, thousands of miles between us.

Out here, churning on the current, I felt very small. The lighthouse stood by itself, alone, and was screened by the low dune hills. There was no trace of Gunwale from this vantage point. As silly as it sounded, in the howling wind and surging water, I felt a little lonely. I had a little time to myself. Who had time for that, anymore?

The beach beckoned. Sunset would be in a little while, so I rode the dinghy into the shore, in the squat-yet-growing shadow of the lighthouse. Being careful to moor the dinghy, I walked ashore and sat down in the sand.

I know, I know, Lou had said I wasn't supposed to be on the beach, that the beaches were off-limits, but considering the overall rule-breaking I was perpetrating, what was another sliver of broken rules added to the stack I'd already accumulated? I didn't like living within limits. Rules were made to be broken.

Overhead there were clouds, fat and puffy-white, billowing things. Walking through the sand, I could see traces of tracks that led their way through the sea oats. I could not guess what they were. There were no birds. I heard only wind. No gulls to be seen, like not a trace.

Maybe I was supposed to find that odd, and maybe I did. But I wasn't a bird expert. Who the hell was I to know where gulls went in their spare time? Did gulls even *have* spare time? Was spare time all that separated mankind from Mother Nature?

The lighthouse was locked up tight, but the light was on, cycling around every three seconds. Taking my phone out, I snapped a shot of it, then another. These days, most lighthouses seemed to be automated. So much was automated. But I wasn't, and I enjoyed capturing these pictures on the sly the way I did. No doubt that nobody local ever walked on these beaches, based on the folks I'd talked to. Maybe I was the first person to have walked around here in awhile.

Up close, I could see scratches on the steel door, marks on the thick chain and padlock, like somebody had been trying to break in. I picked up the heavy chain and ran it through my fingers. Cold steel. I could feel the nicks in the chain links. It looked like the chain had been bitten. I took some pictures of it. Something had savaged the lighthouse chains, and it was hard to be sure what the hell it even was.

The gouges in the door were wider than my hand. I held my hand out and pressed it against the dented door, taking more photographs with my phone.

I sent them to Jade, captioned them: "CHECK THESE OUT."

Looking at the photo, I was less than impressed, and doubted Jade would appreciate them. I mean, it was one of those things you had to be there to fully appreciate. The photo just minimized it, and it seemed inconsequential. But when I saw my hand against that door, and could see those gashes in the steel, the bites on that chain, it was intimidating. Something tried like hell to tear off those chains.

All at once, I felt particularly vulnerable on the beach, in the cool sea breeze, with only the wind and the waves for company. And at that moment, I suddenly became aware of tracks in the sand around me.

Across the dune sand were tracks, crisscrossing along the beach. The beach was covered with them, and not like the ones I'd seen before. I couldn't place the tracks, which looked like maybe they could be pelican prints or something, only bigger. They were webbed feet tipped with claws, and big. Like bigger than my feet. They were easily the diameter of dinner plates.

On a whim, I followed them around, moving back and forth across the beach, trying to get a sense of where they led. The tracks led to Gunwale, over the low hills and sand, toward the harbor. I took photographs of those, as well, but didn't bother sending them to Jade. Those would have bored her even more than my hand shot I'd just taken.

The sun was very low on the horizon, and from Sterner Point, I could see some of the Blackfin ships—sorry, boats—already heading out to sea, cutting their way through the waves, one after another, sailing into the enveloping dark. The setting sun cast the light from yellow, to orange, to amber, catching the fading light as they rode the peaks of the waves.

Where I was, there remained only the restive sea breeze, the soothing and mesmerizing churn of the waves. It would have been the easiest thing in the world to just lay in the sand and watch the night's rise. But I wasn't going to squander the opportunity, having come so far. Having a purpose meant something, and I wasn't going to blow it.

Instead, I shoved the dinghy back into the water, hopped in, and turned on the outboard motor. Above me, the lighthouse shone, the twin beams of light, circling back and forth. It was like a pulsar in its mindless, enigmatic regularity. I knew nobody was searching for me. Nobody but my phone even knew where the hell I even was. There as a kind of thrill in that.

Most of our lives were spent connected in an inextricable web. Where I was, it was just me, the boat, the waves, and the sky.

From where I was, Sterner Point and Gunwale were a sliver of civilization facing a crashing wilderness of waves. I fished out my phone, called up Captain Wayland.

"Hey, I'm out here," I said. "Pick me up. I'm about 300 yards from the lighthouse, East by Southeast."

"Who is this?" Wayland asked, and I felt like maybe he was playing with me.

"It's me," I said. "From the Thirsty Mermaid?"

"Sure. We'll get there, Sport," Captain Wayland said. "Don't move around too much. Stay put. And don't fuck around in the water."

At last the sun vanished beneath the distant horizon, plunging me and everything around me into darkness, except for the lighthouse, which looked like a sunlit candle burning out, with only its ghostly manmade lights whirling like dervishes in the developing darkness.

Something unfamiliar smacked up against the dinghy, distracting me. It was heavy enough to rock the boat. I cranked up the motor on the dinghy and maneuvered into deeper water.

I wasn't sure if there were sharks in this precise part of the coast. I didn't want to know. Sharks were everywhere. What I wanted was for the *Amanda Luce* to come pick me up.

Out at sea, I could see the Blackfin boats with their spotlights on, moving in orderly columns, like a mercantile armada, one after another, fanning out into a wedgelike formation once they're cleared the harbor.

They sounded boat horns, mournful things, speaking to each other, and warning everyone else away.

Something else thumped against the dinghy. I could feel it, could hear it against the metal of the boat. The thump was wet and thick. It had substance.

Then I heard a rasping sound, like something scratching against the metal. The dinghy rocked and turned, while I kept a hand on the throttle, zigzagging the boat. I thought maybe the fishing boats were scaring the fish, the way you sometimes saw bait fish being driven ahead in the water by predators. Only there was an aggressive feeling to the bumps on my dinghy, and I felt like maybe I was the bait fish in this scenario. Sharks sometimes did that, did test bumps against targets, to see if they seemed edible.

But, whatever was bumping the dinghy didn't appear, so I didn't fret about it. I never understood fretting, anyway—as a self-directed man of action, it was an alien emotion that translated in my head to increased awareness, versus worry and, god forbid, anxiety. Jade sometimes wrestled with anxiety in her increasingly rare private moments, but I never did.

Another of the fishing boats had cleared Gunwale's harbor, and looked like it could be heading my way. The dinghy lurched to one side the same time I heard a splash to my left. I could see it, this dripping shape at the edge of the dinghy. In the half-darkness, it was something finned and formidable, judging from how it shifted the weight on the dinghy. But, silhouetted in the uncertain light available to me by way of the fishing boats, I couldn't make out what it was.

Whatever it was, it slipped back into the water with a splash, and the dinghy returned to center. I didn't know what it was. It was wet, and came from the sea. Beyond that, I had no idea. Half-blinded by the flash of spotlights, I couldn't make out what it had been, anyway.

Nightfish, Stupid. That's what you're thinking. No shit. But I didn't know that, yet. In retrospect, yeah. Hell, yeah. It's exactly what it had been. However, at that moment, I didn't know it, yet. I couldn't know it. Hindsight, and all of that.

I gunned the motor again, heading toward the fishing boat that was closest to me, heedless of the hard slap of waves against the hull of the dinghy. The spotlights of the boat illuminated the water around me, turning the inky blue-black to a luminous greenish hue. I could see *Amanda Luce* painted along the bow of the boat.

A line was thrown down, and somebody yelled for me to tie on the dinghy. I quickly tied the bow of the dinghy to the line, and was pulled alongside.

"We should leave the kid in the dinghy," somebody said, one of the backlit shadows aboard the boat. There were several of them, looking down at me with what I imagined was amusement, but was probably more in the neighborhood of mockery. Who did I even think I was? They likely thought I was insane, or, at best, an idiot.

"Front row seat, yeah," another said. The crewmen laughed, like way too hard, and assuredly at my expense.

Somebody rolled down a clattering rope ladder with aluminum rungs, and I climbed aboard, moving up the ladder as quickly as I was able to, without appearing either too eager or too clumsy. The worst thing I could imagine was slipping and falling into the water. Of course, had that happened, that was about the least of my worries.

The nightfishermen gathered around me, a knot of hulking shadows, most of them smoking, all of them carrying bats and axe handles loosely in their thick hands. For a second, I thought I was going to get bludgeoned, but the Skipper emerged from the wheelhouse, looked down at us.

"Gotta hand it to you, Kid," he said. "You've got some stones to come out here at night in that fuckin' dinghy. I know I wouldn't have done that. Not for anything."

"Dinghybat," one of them said, and the others laughed. Even Wayland smirked at me.

"The Dinghybat Shallows," another of them said. "Only babies in these waters. Not even full-grown. Greenbacks for the greenhorn."

They laughed harder, and I felt my face flush. Mindful of the men nearby, mindful of Captain Wayland hanging out above, I looked up at him, tried to be as bold as I could, for I felt that showing weakness in the company of men such as these would be unwise.

"What do you need me to do?" I asked. The boat smelled of oil, soap, rust, steel, and nightfish. I could smell that unmistakably astringent tang over it all, over all the other scents that were marauding my nostrils. This was a working boat, not a cruise ship.

"Nicky," Captain Wayland said. "Get him a smock and a bat. Might as well have him learn it right."

"Nicky" turned out to be a young Portuguese fisherman, who grabbed me by the shoulder and walked me over to a locker area, where he tossed me a bright yellow smock with *Amanda Luce* written on it.

He had an olive complexion and had shaggy brown-black hair that was close-cut in a sloppy tangle around his shoulders. He had tired eyes that none-theless carried mirth in them, despite the seeming fatigue they felt. Nicky gave me some thick gloves, which looked to be made of strong leather, plastic, and quilted plates of steel.

"What are these for?" I asked, turning the gloves over in my hand. They were stained black, like some-body had been finger-painting in ink with them.

"Your hands," Nicky said, cigarette dangling from his lip. Then he fished out two baseball bats, one wood, one aluminum. He held them out for me, those eyes of his blank, like they were made of stone. "You choose."

I never really liked aluminum bats. The sound they made when they hit a ball was less than satisfying. Wood felt purer, more honest. I opted for the wooden bat, still not sure what it was we were doing.

"And the bats?" I asked.

"For *peixe noite.* Nightfish," Nicky said, walking past me with a knowing grin. "We play baseball with them."

—

FIVE

WE WERE ABOUT an hour away from Gunwale, out on the inky black of the ocean, when Captain Wayland turned down the engines, and we just waited a bit on the rolling waters.

Then he barked orders out to the nightfishermen. Out here, the chop of the waves wasn't the gentle motion I'd seen at the shore. It was something else, entirely. Aggressive, like the boat being grabbed and released, over and over again, by the unfriendly, salty paws of an angry sea god. It reminded me of my other fishing outings, but, clutching the bat with those ungainly gloves, it felt somehow worse.

Thankfully, I had a cast-iron stomach. For me, it was maybe a fringe benefit of my cooking experience, but I didn't get nauseous easily. I didn't get motion sick, either. I was grateful for that.

"Man the winches," he said. "Get those nets over, Boys."

The "nets" were these broad spools of metal links, kind of like fencing. There were three in the aft of the Mandy: one dead astern, one at the aft port side, one at the aft starboard side. The winches were strong to carry these loads, and the nightfishermen worked to heave the metal mats over the side, helping to keep them from getting tangled. The noise of it was jarring, as the odd nets scraped the sides of the boat and went down into the water.

The Skipper could see me watching. "They're aluminum, in case you wondered."

"But no hooks," I said. "No bait."

"*We're* the bait, Dinghybat," said the shaggy-haired man, who was working the stern winch. "Nets deployed, Skip."

"Great," Wayland said. Then he went back into the wheelhouse, turned some switch. All at once, there came a pulsing from the Mandy, something I assumed was sonar. It was pinging in a way that made the boat almost tremble, with only the water there to mute the sound. There was something about the sound, something challenging in it. Like the sonic equivalent of someone pounding on a door.

"What's that for?" I asked.

"Helps us see them," the shaggy-haired man said. He was finishing his cigarette, leaning on the handle of the winch.

"It pisses them off," Nicky said. "That's what it does. Even more than the nets."

The men were nervously stepping from one foot to another, were stretching their arms, taking practice swings with their bats. I could see that many of them had nails driven into the heads of their bats. My own bat lacked any nails, and I felt somehow cheated. But I reminded myself that I was only on the Mandy by the grace of Captain Wayland.

The sonar pulses kept going, the Skipper above us, face underlit and green from the scope he was minding. I could see other boats in the distance. All of them had bright lights, pointing seaward. Each boat looked like a bright beacon on a sea of inky black. Pulses were sounding from all of them, like a kind of diabolical chorus.

There was something terrible about the flotilla, the boats bobbing up and down, their spotlights lancing the darkness, their sonar ringing out with relentless pings. And the chain mats, whatever they were, jingled with each rise and fall from the waves. It was a curious sound, unfamiliar to me. For all the noise we were making, we felt so tiny on that surging sea.

"Now what?" I asked.

"We wait," the shaggy-haired man said. "Kid's impatient."

"How come *my* bat doesn't have nails?" I asked.

"You haven't *earned* any nails, Greenhorn," one of the others said, a big man with a black beard, who was carrying a kind of spear that had a backward-curved hook on it. A harpoon, I thought. "On these boats, we have Clubbers, Nailers, Haulers, Spikers, and Cutters. You got no business being a Nailer, so just stay out of the way when *they* come."

"If they come," one of the men said.

"When they come," the black-bearded man said. "They always come."

"Contact," Captain Wayland said from above. "400 meters."

At the words of the Skipper, the men fell silent, and I could see the change in them. Gone were the mumbled conversations and the half-jokes. They tossed aside their cigarettes and gripped their bats. Their faces were fearful and grim. They had broken into three teams of six men each: three Nailers, one Clubber, one Hauler.

"Where do I go, Captain?" I asked.

"You're the Floater," the shaggy-haired man said. "You're goddamned ballast."

"What am I supposed to do?" I asked.

"300 meters," Wayland said. "Big signal, Boys. Kid, you stay out of people's way. You see anything that needs to be hit, you fucking hit it, right? You know how to swing a bat?"

"Should've given him a golf club," the shaggy-haired man said. "Floater, you stay behind us. You see anything fishy, you whack it. You see any gaps in our line, you fill them."

Gaps in lines? Floater? I had no idea what I was going to be doing, and I was nervous as hell. When I got nervous, I talked.

"The nightfish?"

"Yes," he said, like I was an idiot. "The nightfish."

"200 meters," the Skipper said. He got on the radio. "Merlin, this is the Mandy. Stew, we've got a big-ass signal coming here. You boys might want to come on over."

The reply came back garbled, the squawk of the radio and the distance obscuring it, but Captain Wayland seemed to understand, turned on a beacon light at the top of one of the masts of the Mandy, flashing.

The beacon light blinked blue, and some of the other boats sounded their horns, began steaming over to the Mandy's position. Everybody was moving, everything was moving. The chain mats jingled and flexed against their winches, almost striking a kind of beat.

Ching. Ching. Ching-ching. Ching.

Upon seeing that, the nightfishermen called out to each other and became particularly edgy. They formed up at the head of those chain mats, yelling curses at the unseen nightfish, taking more test swings with their bats. Some of them banged their bats on the hull of the Mandy, the aluminum bats ringing out.

"Come on, you bastards!" the shaggy-haired man said.

I'd never seen fishing like this before, had no idea what to expect. I just gripped the bat tightly in my gloved hands and hoped that I'd not make a complete ass out of myself. Another part of me worried that I'd made a terrible mistake coming aboard the Mandy. I didn't belong here, among these nightfishermen.

"100 meters," the Captain said. "Hal, this is the Mandy. I'm thinking we've got maybe 500 head coming up below us, here. How about you guys send some of your boats over here. Plenty enough to go around. We're going to need more bodies to handle this many."

The nightfishermen were now really gearing up, stomping back and forth. I became aware of two more nightfishermen behind me. These were Portuguese men, I could tell from the words they said to each other, which I didn't really understand, but having gone to Carnival down in Rio one year, I knew Portuguese when I heard it. One carried a curved spike in a fist, the other had a machete. They looked at me and grinned.

"*Isca*," one of them said, the one with the spike. He nodded at me. "*O garoto é isca.*"

"*Aposto que eles comê-lo*," the one with the machete said. "*Quer apostar?*"

"*Dinheiro fácil. 10 dólares que ele vai ao mar.*"

"*Feito*," the one with the machete said.

Portuguese was far prettier when spoken by drunk, scantily clad women covered in glitter, sequins, and feathers, dancing to bossa nova beats. Not by a couple of hard-bitten nightfishermen bearing spiked base-ball bats and fearful faces, amid the jingle of chain netting and the harsh sounding of boat horns.

"50 meters," Wayland said. I could see some of the other boats closing in around the Mandy. They turned on their blue beacon lights, too, until they were all flashing. The light played tricks with my eyes, turned the Mandy's crewmen into ghosts, their faces half-lit by the brilliant blue of the beacon, only to lapse back into shadow between pulses of the light. It was dis-orienting, like being in a nightclub from fucking hell. More so when the roll of the boat was thrown into the mix.

"*Isca*," Spike said, as I'd decided to dub the man with the spike. "Don't lose your bat."

"Or your nerve," Machete said. The two men chuck-led, giving each other sidelong glances.

These two men were near a hatch in the deck of the boat, what opened into the hold of the Mandy. There were men belowdecks, too, a half dozen of them with smocks and knives and careworn faces. I did the math. The Mandy had a crew of at least 27 men. I wondered at the price per pound of nightfish to turn a profit, with this many mouths to feed aboard.

"25 meters," the Skipper said. We could feel the Mandy shift a bit, rocking from side to side. "They're on the nets, Boys."

The chain link mats rattled differently and pulled taut, and I could feel that movement. The shaggy-haired man looked at me and smiled.

"Get ready, Kid."

I walked to the starboard side and looked down into the water, illuminated by the great lamps that hung from the booms. I still couldn't see anything, just the tautness of the links and the greenish color of the churning water.

One of the nightfishermen saw me looking. "The light just pisses them off."

"12 meters," Wayland said. "Lordy. At least 500 head. Maybe more. They are packed in tight tonight."

I still couldn't see anything, and then the nightfisherman closest to me shouldered me back. "Get off the line, *Isca*. Back where you're supposed to be."

Chastened, I went back, while the nightfishermen began to shout and point, and I could hear splashing and a horrible hissing sound that I'd never heard before, and the clatter of aluminum chain links. The astringent scent was in the air. It wasn't entirely unpleasant, but it was strange. The scent of nightfish was not unlike iodine.

"There they are," the shaggy-haired man said. "Come on up, you bastards!"

The hissing sounded almost reptilian, like that of a great lizard, but it had other elements to it—a guttural, croaking, bubbling tone that seemed altogether alien. And the hissing came from everywhere, accompanied by splashing. The hissing became louder than the noise of the boats, themselves, louder than the jingling of the chain mats, louder than the shouts of the men. It rose from the sea and enveloped us.

The men at the mats began taking swings with their bats, grunting and yelling, while the hissing continued to grow in volume and intensity. It was a horrible, horrifying hissing, like crazed cats and angry alligators, like a quiver of cobras. All three groups of nightfishermen aboard the Mandy were similarly occupied, and then one of the Haulers called it out, yelling.

"Nightfish 'ho," he yelled, and with a great, winching pivot of his arm, swung this monstrous mass of flesh overhead, slapping it wetly onto the deck. In that moment, I was face to face at last with the enigmatic nightfish.

—

SIX

EVEN LYING ON THE DECK, I could see that the thing was easily as tall as I was, with broad shoulders that rippled with ichthyoid musculature on a bipedal, amphibian-like body. It had smoothly scaly skin and a pair of finned arms that ended in broad, finned hands that looked like catcher's mitts studded with thick, curved claws like fish hooks. The skin was green-black, with stripes that offered some counter-shading along its belly. It smelled of sea salt and fish mingled with that iodine scent.

The face of the thing was easily the most monstrous part of it, with a great toothed mouth and a pair of glowing orange eyes the size of tennis balls, and an array of fins on its head that traveled down its back, and, in this moment, were fully extended as the thing hissed at me, taking angry swipes with its clawed hands. Its face registered no emotion I could fathom, gaping up at me as it fought its way to its feet and then towered above me, my nose barely level with its shoulder.

In that moment, full of uncertainty and terror, I swung at the thing with my bat, as its jaws snapped. It slashed out at me, claws snagging in the heavy apron I wore. Its strength was considerable, and the weight of it pulled me down to the deck. I could feel its cold breath upon me as it tried to bite. The snap of its broad jaws gave me pause. The thing was trying to kill me, and I felt my knees get weak.

"*Morder o mordedor, Isca,*" Spike said, hooking the thing with his curved spike, catching it right in the corner of its mouth, forcing its head over, exposing its neck. "Don't move so much."

Then the man with the machete struck the head off the nightfish with one perfect stroke, spraying me with black blood and sending the head off to the one side, jaws still snapping, big eyes blinking. Spike heaved the headless corpse into the open hatch, dodging its flailing arms. I fought to compose myself, shaking off the stupor and the spray of black blood.

I was shaking. I was rattled.

"Get up, *Isca,*" Spike said.

Another of the Haulers called out, and another one was hauled aboard, then another from the other side. I was swinging with my bat, joined by the other Clubbers, who were pummeling the monsters into submission while Spike and Machete teamed up to lop off their heads.

The things were fighting savagely, scratching, clawing, hissing. The sound of their hissing with the dull thumping of the baseball bats was overwhelming.

"*Isca,*" Spike said. "Take the heads. Throw them overboard."

The deck was already slippery with nightfish blood. I could see the need for getting the heads out of the way, because they did snap and bite reflexively, like the gag store wind-up snapping sets of teeth. Only these were far worse, with those wide-set, bulging eyes and crescent-shaped maws of snapping, triangular teeth. Over and over they snapped, like bear traps, and with more of them being hauled up and beheaded, the number of them kept growing. Piles of nightfish heads, slicks of blood, snapping jaws.

I used the bat, slipping it into the snapping jaws, which would clamp down reflexively on the wood with a crunch, and I would then hurl that head overboard. At this point, so many nightfish were being hauled aboard and bludgeoned that it was a big, bloody blur. I was too scared to think. It was a battle, with each team doing their part, and me having found a kind of role for myself in disposing of the severed heads. There wasn't time to feel anything else. There wasn't even time to think. All I could do was react amid the cacophony of seafaring slaughter around me.

Spike handed me a curved spike of my own, as the bat I'd been using was beginning to splinter from the bites of the nightfish heads. I tossed the bat aside and used the hook to catch the corners of the mouths and toss the heads overboard.

The shaggy-haired guy started calling me "Headhunter" as I went about my grisly task, fetching the snapping heads and tossing them overboard. Gone was any notion of securing some nightfish teeth for Jade as trophies. Gone was any higher brain function, to be honest. I was fueled by adrenalin and terror, scrambling to keep my footing on a blood-soaked and pitching deck, surrounded by the severed heads of nightfish.

"Headhunter's getting the swing of it," one of the nightfishermen said, and I felt almost proud for not making a complete ass out of myself aboard the Mandy, even as I increasingly felt a mix of horror, revulsion, and despair at sight of these nightfish bodies piling up on the deck. There was so much carnage on the deck, it was difficult to comprehend. I slipped and fell three times, was covered in that black nightfish blood in no time.

The shaggy-haired guy looked on and laughed.

"Maybe not completely useless, after all, Headhunter," he said.

And then his throat sprouted a white barbed shard of bone. It happened so fast, he was already yanked overboard before my brain had fully registered what I'd seen.

Something had flashed seemingly out of nowhere and pierced him. Something barbed and deadly. His red blood spurted onto the deck, splashing onto the sea of black blood. It was all that remained of the shaggy-haired guy.

"Harpoons," one of the Haulers said with a baritone bellow that everybody on deck could hear. I heard the Captain call out on the intercom."

"Look out, Boys," Wayland said. "Harpooneers!"

Another of the fishermen caught one of those bony spears, this time in the chest, and I could see a braided kelp line at the tail end of the harpoon go taut and yank the fisherman right over the side in the span of a heartbeat. The harpoons whistled in the air as they flew, thrown with considerable force from somewhere unseen in the water.

The nightfishermen ducked low, while bone harpoons lanced overhead, flashes of white against the night sky. One of them landed at my feet, and I could see the careful, deadly workmanship of the weapon—

the long, pointed end of it meticulously honed, with the back-facing barb rendered with as much care, and engraving along the length of the shaft, with hints of humanoid forms dancing, intertwined, their faces all of a ghoulish, gape-mouthed aspect. The imagery along the weapon was like ghastly scrimshaw, and was, in its way, almost petrifying in the grisly tableau it depicted. The harpoon ended in a bone loop that was braided with the brownish, glistening seaweed.

I wanted to reach for the thing, this Piscean relic, but Spike stopped me with a shout of "*Isca!*"

And I could see all at once that the harpoon suddenly yanked back hard, catching the black-bearded fisherman in the thigh. He bellowed in agony, as he was being pulled overboard by unseen, powerful limbs. Two other nightfishermen went over that way, one of them when a barb caught him in the mouth as it flew back out.

With the line of men momentarily broken by the fusillade of harpoons, more of the nightfish were slipping aboard, clawing and scratching at the men. Great, big, dreadful things, they were, even bigger than the first one I'd seen. They were lean-limbed, but large. Their claws were long, and their mouths were filled with sharp, triangular teeth.

Overhead, I could see Captain Wayland, face still lit green by his scopes, as he gunned the engines of the Mandy, then cursed.

"They've wound something around the props," Wayland said. He reversed the engines.

Meantime, I stood deckside with a half-dozen nightfish, who had already succeeded in hauling two more of the nightfishermen over. A third went over when the nightfish embraced him and simply jumped overboard. I blinked away the man's terrified face, the image painted on the inside of my eyes, just as his forlorn scream echoed in my ears. One moment he was there, and the next moment, he was gone, his scream cut off with a splash.

The Portuguese crewmen kept after the nightfish, to their credit, never once losing their nerve. In fact, Spike produced lances from his workstation and speared some of the nightfish on the ends of those metal poles, holding them so that the Clubbers and Nailers could incapacitate them, before Machete finished them off.

This was more than a harvest or a battle, I decided. It was a war. And, careening on the deck of the *Amanda Luce,* I couldn't tell if we were winning.

The Captain worked the Mandy's engines, trying to unwind whatever it was that the nightfish had used to gum up the propellers. My guess was seaweed, but I didn't want to imagine going down there to find out.

"More harpoons!" hollered one of the Haulers, and everybody ducked again as another salvo of whistling bone harpoons went over the deck, tugging back hard in jerking movements that were terribly effective in snagging bodies. In this case, several of the nightfish themselves were caught and yanked overboard, as well as another of the crewmen.

One of the harpoons had snagged at the lip of the hold, and I grabbed onto it, holding fast to it as the unseen nightfish pulled hard on it. We engaged in a kind of tug-of-war, the nightfish and me.

"*Isca's* on the line," Spike said with a laugh. Machete hesitated for a moment, then chopped the line with the machete.

"You owe me, *Isca*," he said. "Ten dollars."

I had my prize, could feel the carefully carved harpoon in my hand, the surprising weight of it. All along the length of it, the nightfish scrimshaw, depicting their people gathered before a great obelisk that looked almost like a giant pincer. Even in the flashing, disorienting light of the Mandy, I could make out those details on the bone harpoon. I imagined the nightfish harpooner carving the image in the dark with its curved claws.

All at once, something hit me—not literally, thank god—the carvings. Earlier, I had been too dazed to understand it, but now I did.

"Reel in the mats," the Captain yelled on the PA. "Bring them up."

The carvings, harpoons, and braided lines meant culture. Culture meant civilization. Civilization meant intelligence. The nightfish weren't simply animals. They were beings. The weight of that exceeded the heft of the harpoon, itself.

The Haulers, keeping their heads low, turned levers on the winches, which caused the aluminum mats to whirl. The winches were indeed very strong, because there was clearly much more weight on the mats than before.

As the winches groaned, the deck became covered with these fishmen, who stumbled and flopped aboard, attacking, always attacking, without a trace of fear. Their writhing presence filled me with great revulsion. Their great orange eyes gazing about, the strong iodine scent, their teeth snapping and claws clattering on the deck. And the titanic weight of my realization that these creatures—beings—had their own culture. However, in the sloppy, bloody, slippery confines of the deck, there was nothing to do but respond to the chaos around me. There was no time for me to ruminate over my realization.

Instead, I used the harpoon to catch some of them, while Machete went about his ghastly business. Then I'd keep trying to lob the heads overboard, but in the pandemonium of the moment, it was impossible to really have a set routine. It was a desperate battle waged in half-darkness, half-light, full of the scent of sweat, blood, and iodine, with quarter neither asked for nor given. Men screamed and nightfish hissed, boat horns sounded, and always the sound of bats, lances, and machetes against the wet flesh of the nightfish.

One of the deckbound nightfish swung at me with a clawed hand, catching me and sending me to the messy deck, dropping the harpoon. It hissed, glaring at me with its baleful orange eyes. I let out a yelp and kicked at the thing as it reached for me, the two of us locked in a desperate struggle.

Around us, everyone was fighting, and my own battle went on unseen by the crew. The nightfish used its long claws to rend my apron, trying to find purchase in my flesh. It hissed, and I kicked at it with my boots, while trying to swing at it with the curved spike I held tight in my gloved fist.

The nightfish brought its other arm up as I swung with my spike, which pierced its glistening skin. The wound gouted black blood at me. It hissed again, swiped at me with its claws. The look in its eyes was something I would take with me for the rest of my life—it was the darkest, most malevolent hatred. Culture or not, there was hatred in its orange eyes, as it hissed at me. And there was something else, which haunted me even more. There was understanding and antipathy. This was an enemy of humanity, this thing fighting me on the deck. I was as alien to it as it was to me.

And it wanted to kill me. In that moment, we had a shocking intimacy, that awareness that one of us was going to die that night. The nightfish clawed at me, and I attacked the thing with the spike, crying out in terror and desperation as I did so, bashing the life and monstrous light out of the nightfish's eyes, until it writhed and shuddered, ceased hissing, and its clawed limbs went limp.

I paused a moment, fought to catch my breath, and then I bashed it on the head yet again. I got to my feet, my knees and hands shaking, watching the crewmen savage the nightfish, these horrible creatures.

This was a slaughter. I could see the nightfish clambering over the gunwales of the Mandy, cold murder in their glowing eyes. The hissing and the thud of bats, the cries of men, it was all I could hear. The sound and scent of it was enervating. I felt far away from myself, my limbs aching and shaking. Some part of me wanted to run away and hide. However, I didn't let that part of me triumph. I found another part of me, a more savage part of me, and hung onto it for dear life.

Letting out a howl, I dove back into the fray, swinging the curved spike this way and that, as I worked my way back to the harpoon I had dropped. It seemed a cruel joke to attack them with one of their own weapons, but I didn't care. I wasn't me, anymore—I was something else, someone else, fighting for my life on the bloodied deck of the Mandy.

I don't know how long it went on, to be honest. Not moments, but more like forever. Eventually, though, the battle was done, and the last of the nightfish aboard had been taken. Shaking, arms burning, head aching, lungs heaving, I spied some of the triangular nightfish teeth scattered on the deck and shook off a glove, picking them up. Cold to the touch, and devilishly sharp. Some more trophies for me. It felt right to throw them into the sea, back to where they'd come from, but I didn't listen to that particular instinct. Instead, I pocketed them.

Does that make me a bad person? Probably. I did it, anyway. Painted black in nightfish blood, I kept my trophies.

I could see Captain Wayland watching from the wheelhouse. He'd seen me, his face underlit by the scopes he consulted. I could not read his ghostly expression. He seemed a world away from me.

The Mandy had somehow managed to free herself from the propeller tangles the nightfish had attempted, and we were steaming back to Gunwale, the hold bursting with the night's catch, while the sea boiled aft of us, the frenzied nightfish raging in the darkness.

We'd been out for most of the night. One of the younger crewmen, with a boyish face and the Gunwale Look already etched in his eyes, appeared with a hose and was spraying down the deck, washing the black blood off it. A few of the nightfisherman joked that somebody should hose me down, too.

But, overall, the nightfishermen were quiet, now, resting, drinking, smoking. They had lost eight of their number, and were mourning their lost friends. For each one of them understood that it could just as easily have been them.

It could have been me. The thought of it, after the fact, had my knees getting weak again, and I sat down hard on the deck, while the young crewman continued to hose the black blood from the deck with a determination that was admirable. Somebody commented about the sharks trailing our boats, hoping for scraps.

Captain Wayland came out of the wheelhouse and looked me over with a haunted grin.

"Now you know, Kid."

"What are they? What are they, really?"

The Skipper shrugged. "Damned if I know. The old days, they'd come ashore, raided Gunwale. Every night of the full moon, they'd come. So, we just took the battle to them. Can you imagine the first man who ate one of them? Brass balls. I'm betting it was Bob Oakum. That man eats anything he catches."

"They're intelligent," I said. "I saw."

Captain Wayland nodded, giving me a side eye. "Damn right they are. Nightfish aren't what I'd call deep thinkers, but they're not dumb, either."

"I saw," I said. "I saw the carvings on their harpoons. Carvings, man. It looked like, I don't know—religious."

I showed him the harpoon, and Wayland looked it over, turning it this way and that. The iconography was unmistakable. The obelisk, the figures clustered around it. He handed the harpoon back to me, shaking his head.

"I know you saw," Wayland said. He was entirely unruffled. "They're good for Gunwale. They make us money. And back before Blackfin, like I said, they would raid our shores. Nobody believed us. People would just disappear. This is a war, Kid. I don't care what you saw in those eyes. They don't have any use for us except as food. As I see it, we're returning the favor. We're taking the war to them. I grew up in Gunwale. I know the stories. We all knew them. Those things hunt us. The only difference is that Blackfin gives us the opportunity to hunt them back."

I felt terrible. Not just exhausted, but something else. Guilt? Sorrow? Loathing? I don't know what it was. It was a lot of things. I was a mass of confusion. Maybe it was PTSD, I don't know for sure. I could already tell I'd be having nightmares for years because of that night on the *Amanda Luce.*

"It's us or them," Wayland said. "At least around here, it is."

"They're *not* animals," I said.

"That's right," Wayland said. "They're things, Kid."

The iodine scent couldn't be fully washed away, despite the best efforts of the crewman with the hose. I looked at the shredded apron I wore. I was lucky. Not a fucking scratch, despite it all. But I was always lucky that way. I could have easily been snagged by one of those harpoons and yanked overboard, down into the inky dark of the sea. Captain Wayland seemed to read my mind.

"Had you been hooked by one of them, they'd have dragged you down deep," he said. "Maybe you'd have still been alive when they ate you on the way down. I don't know. Nobody they drag down ever comes back up. We just see the blood in the water. Our blood. Some say there are huge nightfish down there—like queens, maybe. Massive ones. They keep growing, the older they get. Bigger, badder, deadlier. Maybe the ones we see hunt to feed their insatiable queens. Maybe they're serving their dark god in the depths. Who knows? I hope I never see it."

It was profane. My gratitude at my own survival, and my dread at what I'd uncovered at Gunwale. Me being me, I was grateful for the experience. I really was. But I was far more grateful that I'd survived it. And there was no way in hell I'd be able to explain it to Jade or anybody else. I didn't know how the night-fishermen could even do it, night after night. Just to feed the insatiable demand for nightfish.

The Captain leaned in, his hard face grown harder.

"You can't tell a soul what you saw here tonight," he said. "Not a fucking soul. People don't want to see *how* it's done, Kid. They only want what they want. They want what we give to them. Yeah?"

"Huh?" I asked. I felt like I was punch-drunk.

"Blackfin keeps people working," Captain Wayland said. "We all have jobs. Good jobs. Good-paying, anyway. You want to take that away from people around here? Fuck that. If I thought you were a squealer, I'd throw you overboard right now. Then you'd see your intelligent nightfish friends up close. They'd get you before the sharks even got a whiff of you. And then where would you be?"

"Dead," I said.

"Fucking eaten. Maybe they'd throw your bones at the feet of their god-queens, or that fucking undersea obelisk as a sacrifice, who knows?" Wayland said. "No, you're not going to tell a soul about this, are you? Not a fucking soul."

"Not a soul," I said, which he took as a promise, because he lit a cigarette, puffed on it reflectively.

"People don't need to know," he said. "And, to be honest—they don't care. They want their nightfish steaks, and we deliver them. You should see it, the way they churn them out at Blackfin. A whole assembly line. Nothing's wasted. I mean, besides those goddamned heads. We process the meat, we grind up the bones for bone meal. The scales for fish food. Nothing's wasted. Not a bit. People—good people—work the factory every shift, processing the nightfish for a world market. Gunwale matters again. Those old fisheries died out, and the nightfish, well, it's a local delicacy that went international. I'm okay with that. I can live with that."

"They're smart," I said, but the Captain only laughed.

"Not smart enough," he said. "C'mon, Kid. You want to be a chef. Have you worked at a slaughterhouse? You ever see a killing floor? Get real. It's no different. Hell, it's worse—the worst a cow can do is maybe stampede you. Nightfish'll kill you first chance they get. I lost eight men tonight, Kid. Eight men. Men with wives and families. That's the most I've ever lost on a run. Tonight's the worst night ever, in terms of that. Some of my men think it's because I brought *you* on board. They think that you jinxed us.

That I should toss you overboard as a sacrifice to the nightfish gods, whatever they are. It's so easy out here. Nobody would ever know. Life and death, Kid. Right here, right now."

His tone told me that he mourned those fallen men. I wondered how many nightfish died that night. I remember he said something like 500 had come up, and did the math—something like one man had died for every 63 nightfish harvested. That was a pretty good ratio, 63-to-1. But I couldn't imagine Captain Wayland having to tell eight families that they'd been lost at sea. I didn't know the men who'd died—I didn't even know the shaggy-haired guy's name, and was afraid to ask Captain Wayland.

"You're a good kid. That's what I told my men, the ones you wanted to toss you overboard," the Captain said. "You'll sort it out, and you'll know that I saved your life tonight, whether you realize it or not."

Then he left me, went to check on his men. They shared some nervous laughter, blew smoke, and took renewed solace in still being alive.

Me, I was in another place, entirely. I couldn't wait to get off that boat. I'd never felt more alone in my entire life.

—

SEVEN

THEY COULDN'T TAKE ME into Blackfin, so when we got close, they had me back in the dinghy, which had somehow managed to survive the harvest intact, and they told me if I told anybody what I'd seen, that somebody would come for me, and that they really would feed me to the nightfish.

"That's a promise, Kid," Captain Wayland said. "Not a threat. More like a fact. Not a word, just like we agreed."

His crewmen laughed, and several of them mimed slitting their own throats, their hard eyes glittering as they gazed at me. I wondered which ones wanted to toss me overboard. From the uniformity of their hard looks, it could have been any of them. I figured it was probably Nicky and Spike, maybe Machete. Sailors were superstitious, and I suppose I understood that. The sea did that. It had a way of putting the fear into a person, irrational and rational braided together, seamlessly interwoven and frayed, as well.

I felt fear again, but a different flavor of fear than I'd first felt on the Mandy.

I didn't want to go back in the dinghy. It felt impossibly small, entirely unsafe, compared with the Mandy, which felt like a fortress. Like a castle, almost.

"Do you lose boats to the nightfish?" I asked Captain Wayland. He looked me over, drinking some strong-smelling coffee from a very well-used white Blackfin mug.

"Of course we do," Wayland said. "Not often, but it happens. We use the mats to draw their attention. So they come at us along routes we want them to. You don't want them swarming your boat from all directions. Besides, they can't really just climb up. We give them a place to go, and they take it. They hate us so bad, they can't help themselves. You get too many on one side, though, and they can capsize your boat. I've seen it happen. *Luden's Folly*, last year. She got swamped by a thousand of them, near as we can tell. I saw it happen. She went right over, went down in minutes. When a boat goes over, you can't even save anybody. The nightfish just swarm them. Blood everywhere in the water. Our blood."

Captain Wayland trailed off, and I could see him seeing that horror, and I could almost imagine it.

"And there's always the queens," Wayland said. "We hear the stories. I've never seen a queen. Hell, I don't think I ever *want* to see one. Stories, you know."

I held out the harpoon to Wayland. It felt cursed to me. I wanted it, but didn't want it, too. I felt like the proper thing would be to lob it into the sea, but I also dreaded the prospect of parting with it, knowing that once it went into the water, I'd never dare to get it back.

"Keep it," Wayland said. "I don't care."

"But it's proof," I said. "Proof of them."

"Nobody'd believe you," he said. "They'll think *you* made it. Hell, we all have ourselves one or two of them. Sometimes folks in town sell them as souvenirs. They call'em scrimshaw. Local flavor. They think we make them locally. Isn't that funny? Nobody ever believed us. Not then, not now. We just haul them in, and that's that."

His men laughed, and I didn't know what they were laughing about. Maybe they were laughing at me, but I couldn't tell. They gave the Captain a wide berth. With eight crewmen down, they knew better than to get in his way.

"If you ever want a job on board the Mandy, there's a spot for you, Kid, if you can find the stomach for it," Wayland said. He took out a nail from his pocket, put it in my palm. It was a thick spike of steel, three inches long. "The harpoon, the teeth you pocketed—those are your trophies. That nail, there—that's your pay, Headhunter. Consider that your share. And, if you get out here again, that'll count as a boarding pass aboard the Mandy, no questions asked. You'd be surprised—you can get a taste for it."

The nightfisherman saw the Captain give me that nail, and began chanting *"Isca!"* and "Headhunter" in equal numbers, until it evolved (or devolved) into *"Isca* Headhunter!" over and over again. Nicky and Spike chattered their teeth at me, clacking them over and over again, while they leered at me. I raised the harpoon at them with each chant, pumping it to the beat. Not out of joy, but defiance. Mock me they might, but I'd survived the night. As had we all. There was something to be said about survival. I just didn't know what.

"Feed him to the fish, Captain," Nicky said. "We still got time."

"Nah," Wayland said. "We're throwing that one back where he came from, Boys. Get off my boat, Kid. But come back anytime."

With those words, like an incantation, the Captain had maybe saved me from his feral crew. It was a salty benediction of sorts, as his men sent me on my way. I pocketed the nail.

Captain Wayland just watched me with those hard, glittering eyes he had, drinking his coffee, while his crew chanted and they helped me off the Mandy and onto my dinghy.

The nightfishermen gave me a mocking bon voyage as I motored away from them with shaking hands. They were taking bets as to whether I'd make it ashore before some stray baby nightfish greenback attacked my dinghy and sent me to the bottom.

I wasn't about to wait to find out. Once I'd removed the line from the Mandy, I motored my way the hell out of there, while they chanted "*Isca* Headhunter" a dozen more times. I stole only one backward glance at the Mandy, because I was determined I'd make it safely back to Gunwale, which required paying attention to where I was going.

That backward glance treated me to a few of the nightfishing fleet in wedge, steaming silhouettes heading back to port, trailed by shark fins, while the sun broke out over the horizon. The *Amanda Luce* looked like a warship, making her way to the safety of the harbor, victorious once more.

—

EIGHT

I RAN INTO Jade in Boston about a week later, and told her everything. She just looked at me like I was nuts, laughed in my face. Even when I showed her the harpoon, she just said it looked like something I'd picked up at a garage sale in New Bedford or something. I had put the thing in my apartment, on the wall, like a trophy. But it didn't feel like a trophy, anymore. It felt like something else. It was something far more grim and significant. It was a relic.

There were days (and nights) when I found myself staring at it, at the tableau upon it, the mysterious, claw-shaped obelisk worshipped by the writhing nightfish, the hand-hewn multitudes etched by an entirely alien clawed hand, with unfathomable intent. I imagined the maker of it in the depths, clawing it in the dark, its great orange eyes alone able to see its efforts. I wondered what compelled it to dress up its harpoon that way.

Maybe it was scrawling what it was seeing. Or maybe it was purely symbolic, invoking its alien god to bring it luck as it hunted the strange surface people in their great alien, shimmering fish that rained down painful noises and mats of metal into their undersea abyss.

Jade didn't care. Whatever I'd experienced in Gunwale was as alien to her as the nightfish themselves were alien to me. I could just see it in her dark eyes, could feel just how done we were.

You didn't see something like I'd seen and come back from it intact, pick right up where you left off; something of it lingered. I showed her the teeth, and she said they looked like shark teeth. She didn't believe a word of it, told me not to forget to pay her back. I made her a necklace out of one of the nightfish teeth, made myself one, too, but when I gave it to her, I could tell in a heartbeat that she'd never wear it. She just thanked me, the picture of polite that spoke volumes to her lack of caring, while I put mine on and never took it off. *Memento mori*—or, memento moray, at the very least.

No matter what, I couldn't get that night out of my head. Before we ended, we'd gone to the Proteus Lounge for dinner, and, of course, they had nightfish on the menu, and Jade ordered it, because she'd gotten a taste for it, after all. The novelty had passed, and now it was simply part of her routine. She could afford it. It was a $200 plate of Nightfish a la Siciliana.

The sight of the raisins, capers, and green olives mingling with the chopped tomatoes and the meat on the plate was just too much. The heady scent of garlic and the iodine tang of the nightfish, I could smell it.

Smell always jogs the memory, and smelling it, I saw that bloody night again. It was the night that had visited me in nightmares that came as regular as the tides. Those orange eyes, the horrid malevolent hissing, unlike anything I'd ever heard. And the blood, absolutely everywhere. Like an obsidian sea.

Me, I couldn't eat it. Couldn't even go there, and Jade could see it, could see me not going there. And I could see her weighing that in her mental scale, and finding me wanting.

"Babe, something really did happen to you out there, didn't it," she said. "You're not right, anymore."

"Guess not," I said. Piles of heads, snapping away, like cadaverous castanets. The screechy jingling of the metal mats, the boat horns, the hissing, the screaming of men, the whistling of the harpoons, the percussive thumping of bats, and the snapping heads, bouncing on the rolling deck. It all came back to me, as if I'd never left. Fuck, I could already see myself in therapy. I mean, I could fucking see it, like I was a prophet. I imagined making a stew out of those horrible nightfish heads, throwing them into a cauldron and boiling them into well-seasoned oblivion—Green Snapper Stew. Or was it Black Snapper? I cracked myself up as I was cracking up. That's where my head went, into a place of pained absurdity.

"You're haunted," Jade said. "That's what you are."

"Am I?" I asked.

"God, yes," Jade said. "I don't like seeing you that way, Babe. You need to be *here*. Like here, with me. Here and now. Right now."

She tapped the table with a lacquered fingernail. Her hair was orange, now. She'd colored it orange, and I couldn't think of anything but them when I saw that color, that shade of orange. Those ghastly eyes.

She forked some of the Nightfish a la Siciliana and downed it with a smile. Not her cocksure smile, but another one. A tentative, reaching smile. A wary smile. A smile that asked why her man would wake up screaming some nights, when he used to sleep peacefully. And why it made me not fun to be around, anymore, whether I was awake or asleep.

"I'm here," I said.

"No, you're not," Jade said. "You need to go, now. Come back when you're *here,* again."

"What's *that* supposed to mean?" I asked. The smell of the nightfish was cloying. No offense to the chef, but they couldn't make it go away, no matter how hard they tried. The stress something felt carried through to the meat when it died. Every nightfish died in horrible battle. That fearsome flavor carried through, at least to me.

I went back to Gunwale three times after that bloody night, months later. I didn't talk to anybody. I just took pictures. Maybe I got obsessed. I don't know. I photographed the Blackfin Fishing Company. I took pictures of their scarred boats.

The Mandy wasn't there the third time I dropped by, right before the end of the nightfishing season. One last haul, before the boats hunkered down and the nightfishermen wintered. I went to the Thirsty Mermaid and asked Rose.

"The *Amanda Luce* sank," Rose said, pointing to the placard on the wall, which showed a picture of the crew, smiling into the camera. Captain Wayland and his crew. Ghosts, now. "All hands aboard were lost. We lost four boats in a storm that night."

"What the hell happened?" I asked.

Harvey and the others raised glasses for the Mandy, muttered to themselves.

"T'was a queen," Harvey said. "Sure as moonlight, but it was. She came up for them, the sea roiling with'em."

The others tried to calm Harvey down, and I couldn't hear over the chatter. Rose looked sad, poured me a whiskey.

"We lose boats now and then in Gunwale," Rose said. "Not usually so many at once, but it happens. Nightfishing's dangerous work. But we're grateful for them that does it. Nightfishing keeps this town alive."

I wondered how it happened. Harvey's words sunk deep into me. Maybe the nightfish had sent a bigger war band. Maybe they had set a trap. Maybe it had been the storm. Maybe it had been all of those things. I imagined the sea churning with them, hell-bent on revenge, a sea of nightfish, watching the boats approach.

I wondered what Wayland thought when they'd taken his boat. I imagined a monstrous nightfish queen, her eyes as big as tractor tires, towering over the boats, with arms thicker than tree trunks, and a maw that could gulp down a car, teeth curved like sabers. A sea monster, she would have been, with a hiss that was more like a bellow.

Up in his wheelhouse, the tide turned, the hissing a chorus, an armada of orange eyes beyond the thick nautical glass. The queen's eyes, like great, bestial orbs alit with malice and revenge. Broken radio, no SOS. Maybe their sheer numbers had caused the Mandy to capsize. Nobody knew. The boats had just disappeared at sea. The Coast Guard had gone looking for them, but had only found some shredded life jackets, no lifeboats. No trace of survivors. All hands lost at sea.

Spokesmen for the Blackfin Fishing Company assured customers and investors that it was only a temporary setback in production, and that they'd resume their harvesting in the spring. Bob Oakum was there on television, making his case. Tanned, handsome, rich, telegenic. Every bit the sea captain he'd once been, with a low voice that commanded attention. His straight teeth were bleached white. Perfectly white, and in that perfection, somehow frightening against the tan of his skin.

Like I said earlier, I woke up from nightmares almost every night. Bolting upright, seeing those things, those goddamned orange eyes, those toothy mouths, those fins and curving claws. The tracks on the beach. Endless tracks, like glyphs on the sand. Searching for what? Prey? Nesting sites? Sacrifices?

I dreamed of them in their underwater world, an army of them off the shores of Gunwale, living in caves, worshipping dark, forgotten gods in the phosphorescent deep. They'd turn their hateful eyes upward, gazing at the luminous boats overhead, pummeling them with sonar, enraging them, wounding them, even, and they would swim for the surface, bearing their harpoons, to fight yet another battle against the soft pink people whose bones littered their caves, piled up at the base of their clawed and godly obelisk.

They were legion, born of phosphorescent orange eggs that lined endless caves and the grottoes that spawned them. Something laid those eggs, and in my nightmare vision, I saw that monstrous sea queen, filling the caves with her eggs. She was huge and horrible, like the nightfish I'd seen, only so much larger. And old. Maybe ancient. A survivor like none other.

Maybe the sea queen really had surfaced to sink those boats. My mind wandered on unfamiliar shores, and I saw her great and terrible form, greater even than I'd imagined before, swamping the Mandy and the other boats, sending them to the bottom, while her children danced on the decks, waving their harpoons, hissing as they feasted on the warm flesh of nightfishermen.

Thousands of them, the nameless things, these nightfish, waiting for the right moonlit night to begin the war along our shores in earnest. Sometime, when the night was right, I knew that I would see them again.

—

FINIS

ACKNOWLEDGMENTS

I would like to thank all of my readers, who offered their time, attention, and opinions to the writing and revision of this novella. I would also like to thank Christine Marie Scott of Clever Crow Design Studio in Pittsburgh for her wonderful cover art and her invaluable assistance with the layout of these pages.

ABOUT THE AUTHOR

Born in Missouri, growing up in Ohio, and settling in Chicago, Dave Neal has always written fiction, but only got really serious about it in the late 90s. He brings a strong Rust Belt perspective to his writing, a kind of "Northern Gothic" aesthetic reflective of his background.

Writing his first novel at 29, he then devoted time to his craft and worked on short stories, occupying a space between genre and literary fiction, with an emphasis on horror, science fiction, and fantasy. He has seen some of his short stories published in "Albedo 1," Ireland's premier magazine of speculative fiction, and he won second place in their Aeon Award in 2008 for his short story, "Aegis." He has lived in Chicago since 1993, and is a passionate fan of music, a student of pop culture, an avid photographer and bicycler, and enjoys cooking.

As D.T. Neal he has published seven novels, *Saamaanthaa, The Happening,* and *Norm*—collectively known as The Wolfshadow Trilogy—*Chosen, Suckage, Return to Summerville* and the cosmic folk horror-comedy thriller, *The Cursed Earth.* He has also published three novellas—*Relict, Summerville,* and *The Day of the Nightfish,* and two collections—*Singularities,* a collection of science fiction stories, and *The Thing in Yellow,* a collection of King in Yellow mythos-based stories.

He is also the co-editor of The Fiends in the Furrows folk horror anthologies: *The Fiends in the Furrows: An Anthology of Folk Horror, The Fiends in the Furrows II: More Tales of Folk Horror,* and *The Fiends in the Furrows III: Final Harvest.*

DTNEAL.COM

ALSO BY D.T. NEAL

NOVELS

Suckage

Chosen

Return to Summerville

THE WOLFSHADOW TRILOGY
Saamaanthaa | The Happening | Norm

Lupinia (A Wolfshadow Book)

NOVELLAS

Relict

Summerville

The Day of the Nightfish

COLLECTIONS

The Thing in Yellow

Singularities

"*Summerville* by D.T. Neal is one of those books that has to be devoured in a single sitting. The story flows incredibly quickly from the 100 page novella, which could have quite easily been stretched out to double its size. Neal however chooses to leave the story with a somewhat ambiguous ending and it works to his advantage beautifully."

—Si, on goodreads.com

D.T. NEAL

RELICT

"So horrifying, and yet so plausible. As an author who has written a book about a giant sea creature, I take my hat off to Neal—this guy takes us all to school in showing what it would be like to be trapped somewhere remote by something with a monstrous size, appetite and intelligence. Great work!"

—Greig Beck, author, on goodreads.com

NOSETOUCH PRESS™

Nosetouch Press is an independent book publisher
tandemly based in Chicago and Pittsburgh.
We are dedicated to bringing some of today's most
energizing fiction to readers around the world.

Our commitment to classic book design in a digital
environment brings an innovative and authentic
approach to the traditions of literary excellence.

*We're Out There™

NOSETOUCHPRESS.COM

Horror | Science Fiction | Fantasy | Urban Fantasy
Mystery | Supernatural | Gothic | Occult | Weird